THE LIGHT OF BETHLEHEM

A Story of Hope and Light

D. DECKKER

Dinsu Books

Copyright © 2024 D. DECKKER

All rights reserved

This book is a work of fiction. The author and publisher assume no responsibility for actions taken by readers based on the content of this book.

No part of this book may be reproduced, or stored in a retrieval system, or transmitted in any form or by any means, electronic, mechanical, photocopying, recording, or otherwise, without express written permission of the publisher.

ISBN-13: 9798301860560

Cover design by: D. DECKKER
Printed in the United States of America

*To my beloved wife, Subhashini, and my precious daughter, Sasha.
Your love, support, and boundless inspiration make every story possible.*

CONTENTS

Title Page
Copyright
Dedication
Preface

Chapter 1: The Angel's Message	1
Chapter 2: Joseph's Dilemma	7
Chapter 3: A World in Chaos	14
Chapter 4: The Magi's Quest	18
Chapter 5: Salome's Skepticism	24
Chapter 6: Herod's Shadow	30
Chapter 7: The Census Decree	36
Chapter 8: The Journey Begins	40
Chapter 9: Danger on the Road	46
Chapter 10: Eli's Revelation	53
Chapter 11: The Magi's Test	60
Chapter 11: The Stranger's Gift	66
Chapter 12: The Arrival in Bethlehem	70
Chapter 13: A Restless Night	75
Chapter 14: Leah's Compassion	79
Chapter 15: Salome's Reluctance	83

Chapter 16: The Birth of Jesus (Part I)	87
Chapter 17: The Birth of Jesus (Part II)	91
Chapter 18: The Shepherds' Night	96
Chapter 19: The Shepherds' Journey	100
Chapter 20: The Magi's Arrival	105
Chapter 21: A Mother's Reflection	110
Chapter 22: The Light Spreads	114
Chapter 23: Herod's Rage	119
Chapter 24: Cassius' Conscience	124
Chapter 25: Flight to Egypt (Part I)	130
Chapter 26: The Massacre Begins	137
Chapter 27: Cassius' Defiance	143
Chapter 28: Flight to Egypt (Part II)	148
Chapter 29: The Magi's Return	154
Chapter 30: Mary's Reflection	158
Chapter 31: The Light of Bethlehem	162
Afterword	169
Acknowledgement	171
About The Author	173
Books By This Author	175

PREFACE

The journey of writing *The Light of Bethlehem* has been one of discovery, reflection, and deep inspiration. It began with a desire to understand and depict not just the iconic story of a miraculous birth, but the humanity, the struggles, and the unwavering hope that paved the way for an event that changed history. Bethlehem, a place often portrayed in simplicity, holds layers of resilience, faith, and the profound light that emerged from such humble beginnings.

This book aims to go beyond what is traditionally known, to offer glimpses into the lives that surrounded that first Christmas—the doubts, the fears, the love, and the sacrifices of those who played their part in this wondrous narrative. Mary and Joseph's journey was not just one of distance but of faith, endurance, and love that overcame impossible odds. The shepherds, the Magi, and even the unknown faces in the crowds—each had a story shaped by that holy night, and it is these stories that form the heart of this book.

As you read, I hope you feel transported into a world of starry nights, flickering lanterns, and whispered prayers. I hope you walk beside Mary as she journeys on dusty roads, feel Joseph's protective strength, and witness the quiet wonder of the shepherds. Above all, I hope you come away with a sense of the light that still radiates from that moment in Bethlehem—a light that has the power to touch hearts, to inspire, and to remind us that miracles often begin in the most unexpected places.

This book is for all who seek hope, for those who believe in love's enduring power, and for anyone who has ever looked up at the stars and wondered about the stories that shape our world. May the light of Bethlehem guide you, warm you, and remind you of the beauty that lies within the simplest of acts and the humblest of beginnings.

CHAPTER 1: THE ANGEL'S MESSAGE

The air was still, the late afternoon sun bathing the small village of Nazareth in a warm glow. Mary's hands were busy, grinding the grain for supper, her thoughts wandering as she worked. The rhythmic scrape of stone against stone filled the quiet of the courtyard, accompanied by the gentle cooing of doves perched on the clay roof. Her mother was inside, humming a hymn, the melody soft and comforting. Everything about the day seemed ordinary, almost sacred in its simplicity.

Mary's mind drifted to her hopes and dreams, thoughts she often entertained while working. She wondered what her future held, whether she would marry soon, and what kind of life awaited her beyond the familiar routines of her home. She cherished the simple joys of her life in Nazareth—her family, her friends, the beauty of the hills surrounding the village. Yet, there was also a yearning within her, a quiet curiosity about the world beyond, about the plans God might have for her. As she ground the grain, her thoughts turned to her cousin Elizabeth, whom she had not seen in a while. Mary hoped she was well, and wondered if she would have the chance to visit her soon.

Suddenly, a rush of wind swept through the courtyard, stirring the dust and sending the doves into flight. Mary looked up, startled, her heart pounding. The air seemed to shift, an unusual stillness descending, as if the world itself was holding its breath. Before her, a figure emerged from the shimmering light, his presence both terrifying and magnificent. His robe glowed like the sun, and his eyes held an unfathomable depth. Mary dropped the stone, her hands trembling as she took a step back.

"Do not be afraid, Mary," the figure spoke, his voice gentle, resonating in the stillness of the afternoon. It was like a melody, calming the fear that had gripped her heart. "You have found favor with God."

Mary's lips parted, her breath caught in her throat. She felt as though time had slowed, the world narrowing to this single moment. The angel's presence filled the courtyard, an otherworldly light radiating from him. She wanted to speak, to ask who he was, why he had come—but her voice failed her.

"You will conceive and give birth to a son," the angel continued, his gaze never wavering from hers, "and you are to call him Jesus. He will be great and will be called the Son of the Most High. The Lord will give him the throne of his father David, and he will reign over Jacob's descendants forever; his kingdom will never end."

Mary's mind raced, the words echoing in her ears. A son? The Son of the Most High? It was too much to comprehend, a weight she could scarcely carry. Her hands moved to her abdomen instinctively, her fingers brushing against the fabric of her tunic. She had known no man—how could this be?

She swallowed, her voice barely a whisper as she spoke. "How will this be, since I am a virgin?"

The angel's expression softened, a warmth emanating from him that seemed to reach into her very soul. "The Holy Spirit will come upon you, and the power of the Most High will overshadow you. So the holy one to be born will be called the Son of God. Even Elizabeth, your relative, is going to have a child in her old age, and she who was said to be unable to conceive is in her sixth month. For no word from God will ever fail."

Mary's heart swelled with a mixture of awe and fear, her thoughts spinning. Elizabeth—pregnant? She could scarcely believe it. And yet, here was this being, this angel, telling her that she, too, had been chosen for something beyond her understanding. Her entire life, she had been taught to trust in the Lord, to have faith even in the face of uncertainty. But this—this was different. This was a call to faith that went beyond anything she had ever imagined.

She looked up at the angel, her eyes wide, her heart pounding. Slowly, she sank to her knees, her voice steady despite the tremor in her hands. "I am the Lord's servant," she said, her words filled with quiet conviction. "May your word to me be fulfilled."

The angel smiled, a light of pure joy radiating from him, and in an instant, he was gone. The courtyard was still once more, the doves returning to their perch, the air settling around her. Mary remained kneeling, her heart heavy with the weight of what had just happened. She closed her eyes, taking a deep breath, her fingers brushing the ground beneath her as if to steady herself.

Slowly, she rose to her feet, her mind a whirlwind of thoughts. She knew she had to tell her mother, but how could she put into words what had just occurred? How could she explain the feeling of divine presence, the call that had been placed upon her life? The fear, the awe, the responsibility—it all pressed down on her, yet beneath it, there was also a sense of peace. A sense that somehow, this was meant to be.

She stepped into the house, her eyes adjusting to the dim light inside. Her mother looked up from her work, her eyes softening when she saw Mary. "You look pale, child," she said, concern lacing her voice. "Are you feeling unwell?"

Mary opened her mouth to speak, but no words came. Instead, she moved to her mother's side, kneeling before her and resting her head in her mother's lap. Her mother's hand came to rest on her hair, stroking it gently, the familiar gesture bringing comfort. Mary closed her eyes, her heart pounding as she tried to find the words.

"Mother," she began, her voice barely above a whisper, "something… something happened today."

Her mother's hand paused, and she looked down at Mary, her brow furrowed. "What is it, my dear?"

Mary lifted her head, her eyes meeting her mother's. There was fear there, yes, but also a quiet determination. She took a deep breath, her voice steady as she spoke. "An angel came to me. He said… he said that I will bear a son. The Son of God."

Her mother's eyes widened, her hand coming to rest over her heart. For a moment, there was only silence between them, the weight of Mary's words settling in the small room. Her mother's gaze searched Mary's face, and slowly, she nodded, her eyes filling with tears.

"The Lord has chosen you," she whispered, her voice thick with emotion. "My child… what an honor, what a blessing."

Mary felt tears prick at her own eyes, and she reached for her mother's hand, holding it tightly. "I'm scared, Mother," she admitted, her voice trembling. "I don't know if I'm strong enough for this."

Her mother cupped Mary's face in her hands, her eyes filled with love. "The Lord would not have chosen you if you were not strong enough," she said, her voice firm. "You are brave, Mary. You have always been brave. And you are not alone. We will face this together."

Mary nodded, a tear slipping down her cheek. She closed her eyes, resting her forehead against her mother's, drawing strength from her words. In that moment, she knew that no matter what lay ahead, she would not face it alone. She had her family, her faith, and the quiet, unwavering belief that somehow, everything would be alright.

* * *

The sun dipped below the horizon, the courtyard bathed in the soft glow of twilight. Mary stood at the doorway, her eyes fixed on the first stars beginning to appear in the evening sky. The angel's words echoed in her mind, a constant reminder of the path that lay before her. She felt the weight of it, the uncertainty of what was to come—but there was also hope. A hope that maybe, just maybe, this child she carried would bring light to a world that so desperately needed it.

She took a deep breath, her hand resting on her abdomen. She could feel the life growing within her, a tiny spark that filled her with both fear and wonder. She knew the road ahead would not be easy, that there would be challenges she could not yet imagine. But she also knew that she had been chosen for a reason, that her faith would guide her through whatever lay ahead.

A rustle of movement behind her made her turn, and she saw her father standing in the doorway, his eyes filled with quiet pride. He stepped forward, his hand resting on her shoulder. "Your mother told me," he said, his voice low. "I want you to know that we are with you, Mary. Whatever happens, we will be by your side."

Mary looked up at him, her eyes shining with unshed tears. "Thank you, Father," she whispered, her voice thick with emotion. She reached up, covering his hand with her own. In that moment, she felt a sense of peace, a sense of belonging. She was not alone. She had her family, her faith, and the knowledge that she was part of something far greater than herself.

As the stars continued to fill the sky, Mary stood with her father, her heart filled with a quiet, steady determination. She didn't know what the future held, but she knew one thing for certain: she was ready to face it. Whatever came, she would face it with courage, with faith, and with the unwavering belief that she had been called for a purpose. And that, no matter how uncertain the path ahead, she would not walk it alone.

CHAPTER 2: JOSEPH'S DILEMMA

The sharp sound of a hammer hitting wood echoed through the small workshop, its rhythmic beat filling the otherwise quiet space. Joseph's hands moved with practiced precision, the muscles in his arms flexing as he worked. His thoughts, however, were anything but focused. They spun in a chaotic loop, always circling back to the same impossible truth—Mary was with child. The woman he loved, the woman he was to marry, was pregnant, and it was not his.

He paused, letting the hammer fall to his side, his chest tightening with a mix of confusion and pain. The scent of freshly cut cedar filled the air, but even that familiar comfort could not ease the ache inside him. He closed his eyes, his brow furrowed, and tried to steady his breath. He had always known Mary to be a woman of integrity, her faith unwavering, her heart pure. The thought of betrayal seemed impossible, yet the evidence was undeniable.

Joseph began to pace restlessly, his feet moving across the wooden floor as his thoughts swirled in turmoil. He ran a hand through his hair, his heart pounding in his chest. He tried to focus on his work, to lose himself in the familiar rhythm of carpentry, but his hands trembled, the tools slipping from his grasp. The hammer clattered to the ground, the sharp noise echoing in the quiet room. He bent to pick it up, his fingers shaking, his frustration mounting. How could he make sense of any of this? How could he reconcile what Mary had told him with what he knew to be true?

"Joseph?" a voice called, breaking through his thoughts. He looked up to see his brother, Samuel, standing in the doorway, his expression concerned. "You've been out here for hours. Is everything alright?"

Joseph forced a smile, though it felt hollow. "I'm fine, Samuel. Just... needed some time to think."

Samuel studied him for a moment before nodding slowly. "Alright. But you know, if something's bothering you, I'm here to help." He hesitated, then added, "You're not alone, brother."

The words struck a chord deep within Joseph, and he nodded, though he couldn't bring himself to respond. Samuel lingered for a moment longer before turning and leaving the workshop, the door creaking softly as it closed behind him. Joseph set the hammer down on the workbench, his fingers brushing against the smooth grain of the wood. He had always taken pride in his work, in the tangible results of his labor. But this—this was something he couldn't fix with his hands. This was something far beyond his control.

The sun had begun to dip below the horizon, casting a warm golden light through the small window. Joseph sank onto a stool, his head in his hands. He wanted to believe Mary, to trust her as he always had. But how could he reconcile her words with what he knew to be true? She had told him of an angel, of a message from God—but it sounded like something out of a dream, a story too fantastical to be real.

His heart ached at the thought of her, her gentle smile, the way her eyes lit up when she spoke of her faith. He loved her—he had always loved her. He remembered the first time he had seen her, her laughter as she played with the children in the village, the kindness in her eyes when she spoke to those in need. She had always been so full of light, so full of hope. And yet, the doubt gnawed at him, an unwelcome presence that refused to be silenced. He had thought about ending their engagement, about quietly stepping away to spare them both the shame and ridicule that would surely follow. But the thought of leaving her, of abandoning her in her time of need, was almost more painful than the betrayal he felt.

A soft knock on the door pulled him from his thoughts, and he looked up to see his mother standing in the doorway, her eyes filled with concern. "Joseph, dear," she said gently, "it's getting late. You should come inside."

Joseph managed a small smile, though it didn't reach his eyes. "I will, Mother. Just… a little longer."

She nodded, her gaze lingering on him for a moment before she turned and left. Joseph watched her go, a heaviness settling in his chest. He knew his family was worried about him, that they could see the strain he was under. But how could he explain what he was feeling when he barely understood it himself?

As the last light of day faded, Joseph rose from the stool, his movements slow and deliberate. He made his way to the small cot in the corner of the workshop, his body weary from the weight of his thoughts. He lay down, his eyes fixed on the ceiling, the darkness pressing in around him. He closed his eyes, his heart aching with the uncertainty of what lay ahead.

Sleep came slowly, his mind a tangle of thoughts and emotions. And then, in the quiet of the night, a light appeared—a soft, gentle glow that seemed to fill the entire room. Joseph's eyes opened, his breath catching in his throat as he saw a figure standing before him. The man's presence was radiant, his robes shimmering like the light of the moon, his face serene and kind.

"Joseph, son of David," the figure spoke, his voice calm and reassuring, "do not be afraid to take Mary as your wife, for what is conceived in her is from the Holy Spirit. She will give birth to a son, and you are to give him the name Jesus, because he will save his people from their sins."

Joseph's heart pounded, his eyes wide as he stared at the angel. The words echoed in his mind, a sense of peace washing over him that he hadn't felt in days. The doubt, the fear, the confusion—it all seemed to fade away, replaced by a quiet certainty. He could see Mary's face in his mind, her eyes filled with hope and love, and he knew, without a doubt, that she had been telling the truth.

The angel's light began to fade, and Joseph reached out, as if to hold onto the moment, to hold onto the peace that filled him. "Wait," he whispered, his voice barely audible. "How… how can I do this? How can I protect them?"

The angel paused, his gaze meeting Joseph's, a gentle smile on his lips. "You are not alone, Joseph. The Lord is with you, and He will guide you. Trust in Him, and He will give you strength."

Joseph felt tears prick at his eyes, a warmth spreading through his chest. The angel's words resonated deep within him, a reassurance that seemed to fill every corner of his being. He nodded, his voice barely a whisper. "Thank you."

The angel's form slowly dissolved into light, the room once again dark and still. Joseph lay there for a moment, his breath coming in shallow gasps, his heart pounding in his chest. Slowly, he sat up, his eyes adjusting to the darkness. The workshop was silent, the only sound the gentle rustle of the wind outside. He pressed a hand to his chest, feeling the steady beat of his heart, the warmth that still lingered from the angel's presence. He knew what he had to do. He had to trust Mary, to stand by her, no matter what others might say or think.

He rose from the cot, his movements purposeful as he crossed the room and opened the door. The night air was cool against his skin, the stars scattered across the sky like a thousand tiny lanterns. He took a deep breath, his gaze fixed on the horizon, a sense of calm settling over him. He would not abandon Mary. He would be by her side, no matter the cost.

The next morning, Joseph made his way to Mary's home, his heart steady, his mind clear. He knocked on the door, his breath catching as he waited. The door opened, and there she was—Mary, her eyes wide with surprise, her hands trembling slightly as she looked at him.

"Joseph," she breathed, her voice barely a whisper. "What are you doing here?"

He stepped forward, his eyes meeting hers, the love he felt for her overwhelming the doubt that had once clouded his heart. "Mary," he said, his voice steady, "I believe you. I believe what the angel told you. And I will stand by you, no matter what. I will marry you"

Tears filled her eyes, her hand coming to rest over her mouth as she tried to hold back a sob. "Oh, Joseph," she whispered, her voice breaking. She reached for him, her fingers brushing against his, and he took her hand, holding it tightly.

"We will face this together," he said, his voice filled with quiet determination. "You are not alone. I am with you."

Mary nodded, her tears spilling down her cheeks, and she stepped forward, wrapping her arms around him. Joseph held her close, his heart swelling with a sense of purpose, of love. He knew the road ahead would not be easy, that there would be challenges they could not yet imagine. But he also knew that they were not alone, that they had each other, and that they would face whatever came their way together.

As they stood there, holding each other in the early morning light, Joseph felt a sense of peace wash over him. The fear, the doubt, the uncertainty—it was still there, lingering in the corners of his mind. But it no longer held power over him. He had made his choice, and he would walk this path with Mary, no matter where it led.

The sun began to rise, casting a golden glow over the village, and Joseph knew that this was just the beginning. There would be trials, there would be hardships, but there would also be love, and hope, and the promise of something greater than themselves. And that, he thought, was enough.

※ ※ ※

Later that day, Joseph and Mary sat together in the small courtyard, the warmth of the sun on their faces. Mary's hand rested on her abdomen, a soft smile playing at her lips. "Do you think he will look like you?" she asked, her voice filled with wonder.

Joseph chuckled, his eyes crinkling at the corners. "I hope he has your eyes," he said, his voice gentle. "Kind and full of light."

Mary looked at him, her eyes shining with love. "And I hope he has your heart," she said softly. "Brave and true."

Joseph reached for her hand, lacing his fingers with hers. "Whatever he is, whoever he becomes," he said, his voice filled with quiet conviction, "he will be loved. And we will do everything we can to protect him."

Mary nodded, her heart swelling with emotion. She knew the path ahead would not be easy, that there would be challenges they could not yet foresee. But she also knew that they were not alone, that they had each other, and that they would face whatever came their way with faith and love.

As the sun dipped below the horizon, casting a warm glow over the village, Joseph and Mary sat together, their hands intertwined, their hearts filled with hope for the future. They knew the journey ahead would be difficult, that there would be moments of doubt and fear. But they also knew that they had been called for a purpose, that their love and their faith would guide them through whatever lay ahead.

And as the first stars began to appear in the night sky, Joseph looked at Mary, his heart filled with a quiet, steady determination. He would stand by her, no matter what. He would protect her, and the child she carried, with everything he had. And he knew, deep in his soul, that they were part of something far greater than themselves—a story that was only just beginning.

CHAPTER 3: A WORLD IN CHAOS

The sky was overcast, a heavy gray that seemed to press down on the village of Nazareth, mirroring the mood of its people. Roman soldiers marched through the streets, their armor glinting dully in the weak sunlight. The villagers watched them pass, their eyes filled with a mixture of fear and resentment. Life under Roman rule was harsh—taxes were high, food was scarce, and the constant presence of soldiers was a reminder of their powerlessness. But beneath the fear, there was something else—a quiet, desperate hope.

Eli and Abram stood near the well, drawing water as they listened to the murmurs of those around them. A group of women gathered nearby, their voices hushed as they spoke of the latest rumors. "The elders say a savior is coming," one of them whispered, her eyes glancing nervously at the soldiers. "Someone who will free us from this oppression."

Abram exchanged a glance with Eli, his brow furrowed. The elders had spoken of a savior for as long as he could remember, but lately, it seemed as though more and more people were clinging to that hope. He watched as a young mother, her child clutched to her chest, whispered a prayer under her breath, her eyes closed in fervent hope. It was moments like this that made the prophecy feel real—tangible. The belief in a coming savior was not just a story; it was the thread that held their community together, a promise of deliverance from the weight of Roman rule.

As they filled their buckets, Eli and Abram overheard a group of men speaking in low voices near the market. "The Romans took another cart of grain this morning," one of them said, his voice tight with anger. "How much longer can we endure this?"

"We have to trust in the prophecy," another man replied. "The elders say a savior is coming—someone who will lead us out of this darkness."

Eli felt a surge of emotion—hope mixed with frustration. He wanted to believe in the prophecy, but each day seemed to bring new hardships, new reminders of their powerlessness. He glanced at Abram, who nodded, his expression somber. "We must hold on," Abram said quietly. "It's all we have."

A sudden commotion near the edge of the village drew their attention. Roman soldiers were shouting, their voices harsh as they confronted a group of shepherds. Eli and Abram hurried over, their hearts pounding as they pushed through the gathered crowd. One of the soldiers had a shepherd by the arm, his grip tight as the man struggled to free himself.

"You think you can defy Rome?" the soldier spat, his eyes cold. The shepherd's face was pale, his eyes wide with fear, but there was a spark of defiance there as well—a refusal to be broken.

Abram clenched his fists, his jaw tight as he watched. The villagers stood by, their faces a mix of fear and anger, but no one moved to intervene. They knew better than to draw the soldiers' attention. Eli felt his heart ache with helplessness, the weight of their situation pressing down on him. How long could they endure this? How long before something—someone—brought an end to their suffering?

After what felt like an eternity, the soldier released the shepherd, shoving him to the ground. The crowd let out a collective sigh of relief as the soldiers moved on, their heavy footsteps echoing in the stillness. Eli and Abram helped the shepherd to his feet, their eyes meeting in a silent understanding. They were all in this together, bound by the same hope, the same longing for freedom.

As they walked back toward the well, Abram spoke, his voice low. "The prophecy... it has to be true. There has to be something more than this."

Eli nodded, his heart heavy. He thought of his family, of the children who deserved a better life than this. He thought of the elders, their voices steady as they spoke of the savior who would come to deliver them. And he thought of Mary—gentle, kind Mary—who had always believed in the promise of something greater. He wanted to believe too, wanted to hold onto the hope that one day, their suffering would end.

That night, as the village settled into an uneasy quiet, Eli knelt beside his bed, his hands clasped in prayer. He closed his eyes, his voice barely a whisper as he spoke. "Lord, if you are listening, if the prophecy is true... please, send us the savior. We cannot endure this much longer."

The wind rustled through the trees outside, the only sound in the stillness of the night. Eli remained there for a long time, his heart aching with the weight of his plea. He knew he was not alone—knew that across the village, others were praying too, their voices lifted in a quiet, desperate hope. They were waiting, yearning for the day when the prophecy would be fulfilled, when their world would be made whole again.

The next morning, as the first light of dawn broke over the hills, Eli and Abram stood at the edge of the village, their eyes fixed on the horizon. The air was still, the world bathed in the soft glow of morning. They knew the road ahead would be difficult, that there would be more hardships, more struggles. But they also knew that they were not alone—that they were part of something greater, something that would one day bring them the freedom they longed for.

Eli took a deep breath, his heart filled with a quiet determination. They would hold on to the hope of the prophecy, would cling to the promise of a savior. And until that day came, they would endure—together, as a community, bound by their faith and their longing for deliverance.

CHAPTER 4: THE MAGI'S QUEST

"Azar, look! The star has appeared again!" The voice of Master Balthazar was filled with excitement, his eyes fixed on the night sky, where a brilliant light blazed against the dark canvas of the heavens. Azar followed his master's gaze, his eyes narrowing as he looked up. The star was undeniably bright, its light shimmering with a kind of intensity that seemed almost unnatural. The other magi, Melchior and Gaspar, stood nearby, their faces alight with awe and conviction.

Azar shifted on his feet, his heart pounding as he tried to feel the same sense of wonder that radiated from the others. He was young, barely twenty, and had always been the one to question, to doubt. His mentors spoke of signs and prophecies, of a great king who would be born under the light of this star. But as he stared at the sky, all Azar could feel was uncertainty. The desert wind was cool against his skin, the scent of sand and spices filling the air, but even that familiar comfort could not quiet the doubts that stirred within him.

Melchior stepped closer, his eyes filled with reverence. "It is the sign we have been waiting for," he said, his voice deep and resolute. "The prophecy is being fulfilled, and we must follow it. We must find the child."

Azar's gaze flickered between the star and the faces of his mentors. He wanted to believe, but his skepticism held him back. His thoughts churned, questioning the possibility of such a miracle. How could a star lead them to a king? His brows furrowed as he looked at Melchior, the older man's face lined with age and wisdom.

"Are we sure?" Azar asked, his voice hesitant. He tried to mask his doubt, but it seeped through in the way his eyes darted away, the way he shifted uneasily. "Are we sure that this is the sign we've been waiting for?"

Balthazar turned to him, his eyes softening. He placed a hand on Azar's shoulder, his touch gentle but firm. "Faith, Azar," he said quietly. "Faith is not always about what we see or understand. Sometimes, it is about what we feel in our hearts. Do you not feel it? The call of something greater, something beyond ourselves?"

Azar clenched his jaw, his eyes drifting back to the star. It was beautiful, there was no denying that. Its light was pure, almost ethereal, and as he stared at it, he felt a flicker of something deep within him—a pull, a whisper that seemed to echo in his very soul. He rubbed the small pouch of herbs at his belt, a habit he had developed when he was uncertain, his fingers seeking comfort in the familiar texture.

"I want to believe," he said, his voice barely audible. "But it's hard. How can a star lead us to a king? How can we be sure that this is real, and not just... wishful thinking?"

Gaspar stepped forward, his eyes kind as he looked at Azar. He clasped his hands behind his back, his voice gentle. "It is not wrong to question, young one," he said. "Questions lead us to truth. But sometimes, we must also be willing to take a step into the unknown, to trust in something greater than ourselves. The star is a sign, Azar. A sign that something miraculous is happening, something that we have been waiting for our entire lives."

Azar nodded, though his heart was still heavy with doubt. He watched the others, their faces illuminated by the star's glow, their eyes filled with hope and determination. The conviction that burned within them seemed almost tangible, a force that propelled them forward. He wanted to trust them, to share in their hope. He glanced at the star again, its light pulsing with a strange vitality, as if it were beckoning them onward.

"We leave at dawn," Balthazar said, his voice filled with quiet determination. "We will follow the star, and we will find the child. The journey will be long, and it will not be easy. But we are called to this, and we must see it through."

Azar swallowed, his eyes still fixed on the star. It seemed to pulse with light, as if it were alive, as if it were watching them. He took a deep breath, his heart pounding in his chest. He didn't know what lay ahead, didn't know if this journey would lead them to the truth they sought. But he knew one thing—he could not stay behind. He had to see this through, to find out for himself if the stories were true.

"I will come," he said, his voice steady, though his heart still wavered. "I will follow the star."

Balthazar smiled, his eyes filled with pride. "Good," he said. "Then let us prepare. We have a long journey ahead of us."

※ ※ ※

The dawn was cool, the sky painted in hues of pink and gold as the magi set out across the desert. Azar rode alongside his mentors, the camels' steady gait a comforting rhythm beneath him. The sand stretched out before them, endless and golden, the sun just beginning to rise above the horizon. The star still shone in the early morning light, its brilliance undiminished, guiding them eastward.

Azar's thoughts were a tangle of hope and fear, his eyes flickering between the star and the vast expanse of desert before them. He could hear the soft murmur of his mentors' voices as they spoke of the prophecies, their words filled with excitement and reverence. He wanted to share in their joy, to feel the same sense of purpose that drove them. But doubt still lingered, a shadow that refused to be banished.

"Azar," Gaspar called, drawing his attention. The older man rode beside him, his eyes filled with warmth. "You seem troubled, my boy. Speak your mind."

Azar hesitated, then sighed, his gaze dropping to the reins in his hands. "I just... I don't know if I'm ready for this," he admitted. "What if we're wrong? What if this star leads us nowhere, and all of this is for nothing?"

Gaspar nodded, his expression thoughtful. "Those are fair questions," he said. "But tell me, Azar—what if we are right? What if this star leads us to something beyond our wildest dreams? To a king who will bring hope to the world? Is that not worth the risk?"

Azar looked up, his eyes meeting Gaspar's. There was a kindness there, a wisdom that went beyond words. He could see the belief that burned within the older man, a belief that had carried him across countless miles, through years of searching and waiting. And in that moment, Azar felt a flicker of something —something that felt like hope, like the first rays of sunlight breaking through the darkness.

"I suppose it is," he said, a small smile tugging at his lips. "I suppose it's worth it."

Gaspar smiled, reaching over to place a hand on Azar's shoulder. "That's all we can ask for, my boy. To be willing to take the journey, even when we are unsure of where it will lead."

Azar nodded, his heart feeling a little lighter. He looked up at the star, its light shining bright against the morning sky. Maybe, just maybe, there was something to all of this. Maybe the stories were true, and they were being led to something miraculous. He didn't know for sure, but he was willing to find out. And that, he thought, was enough for now.

* * *

Days turned into weeks as they traveled, the desert stretching out before them, endless and unforgiving. The sun blazed during the day, the heat oppressive, while the nights were cold, the wind biting against their skin. But the star remained, a constant presence in the sky, guiding them onward. Azar found himself growing accustomed to the rhythm of the journey, the steady pace of the camels, the quiet conversations with his mentors as they made camp each night.

One evening, as they sat around the fire, Balthazar spoke of the prophecy once more, his voice filled with reverence. "A child, born under the light of a star," he said, his eyes reflecting the flames. "A king who will bring hope to the world, who will lead us out of darkness. We are witnessing something extraordinary, my friends. Something that will change the course of history."

Azar listened, his eyes fixed on the fire, the warmth of the flames a welcome comfort against the chill of the night. He still struggled to believe, still found himself questioning the truth of it all. But there was something in Balthazar's voice, something in the way his mentors spoke of the child, that made Azar want to believe. He looked up at the star, its light unwavering, and felt that familiar pull deep within him.

"Do you ever doubt?" he asked, his voice quiet. The others turned to look at him, their expressions softening. "Do you ever wonder if we're wrong?"

Melchior smiled, his eyes kind. "Of course, Azar," he said. "We all have our moments of doubt. But faith is not about being without doubt. It is about choosing to move forward, even when we are uncertain. It is about trusting in something greater than ourselves."

Azar nodded, his heart swelling with a mixture of hope and fear. He looked at the star once more, its light a beacon in the dark sky.

He still didn't know if they were right, still didn't know if this journey would lead them to the truth they sought. But he knew one thing—he was willing to see it through, to follow the star to the end, wherever that might be.

And as the fire crackled softly, the desert stretching out around them, Azar felt a sense of peace settle over him. The journey was far from over, and the road ahead was uncertain. But he was not alone. He had his mentors, his friends, and the light of the star to guide him. And that, he thought, was enough.

* * *

The next morning, they set out once more, the sun rising over the desert, the sky painted in hues of orange and pink. The star still shone, its light guiding them onward, and Azar felt a sense of determination settle in his heart. He didn't know what lay ahead, didn't know if they would find the child they sought. But he knew one thing—he would follow the star, he would see this journey through to the end.

As the camels moved steadily across the sand, Azar looked up at the sky, the star a constant presence above them. And for the first time, he allowed himself to hope—truly hope—that they were being led to something miraculous, something that would change everything.

"We're coming, child," he whispered, his voice carried away by the wind. "We're coming to find you."

CHAPTER 5: SALOME'S SKEPTICISM

"Miracles," Salome scoffed, her voice edged with bitterness as she set her basket down on the dusty ground. The scent of herbs—lavender, thyme, and a hint of sage—wafted into the air as she knelt beside a young woman, her hands already working to assess the woman's swollen belly. Salome's fingers moved with practiced ease, her touch sure, but her eyes remained hard, her expression unyielding.

Miriam, her eyes wide with a mixture of fear and hope, looked up at the older woman, her lips trembling. "The elders say a king is coming," she said, her voice barely a whisper. "They say a star has appeared in the sky, that a child will be born to save us."

Salome rolled her eyes, letting out a sharp sigh as she continued her examination. "They say a lot of things, child," she muttered, her voice laced with skepticism. "But talk is just talk. Words will not put food on your table or keep you safe from Roman soldiers."

Miriam's eyes filled with tears, her gaze dropping to the ground. Salome paused, her own heart tightening at the sight of the young woman's despair. She had seen it too many times—the hope that shone in a mother's eyes, only to be extinguished by the harshness of life. She had once believed in miracles, too, had once thought that there was something greater than the suffering they endured. But those days were long gone, buried beneath years of loss and heartache.

"I'm sorry," Salome said, her voice softening, though the edge of cynicism remained. She turned her gaze away, focusing on the herbs in her basket. "I don't mean to take away your hope. It's just... this world is hard, Miriam. And sometimes, it feels like hope is a luxury we can't afford."

Miriam nodded, her tears spilling down her cheeks. "I just want my child to be safe," she whispered, her voice cracking. "I want him to grow up in a world that is better than this."

Salome's chest tightened, and she looked away, her fingers stilling on Miriam's belly. She had wanted the same thing once. She had wanted a world where her own child could grow up without fear, without the ever-present shadow of Roman oppression. But that dream had died the day her child had been taken from her, the day the hope she had held onto so tightly had slipped through her fingers like sand.

"I know," Salome said, her voice barely audible. "I know you do."

She finished her examination, her hands moving with mechanical precision as she helped Miriam sit up. The young woman offered her a watery smile, her eyes still filled with that fragile hope that made Salome's heart ache. Salome turned away, gathering her herbs, her fingers brushing against the soft leaves, the scent filling her senses. It was a small comfort, the only solace she had left.

"Rest, Miriam," she said, her voice brusque as she stood. "You need your strength for the days ahead. And remember, no matter what they say about kings and stars, it is your own strength that will see you through."

Miriam nodded, her eyes still glistening with tears. "Thank you,

Salome," she whispered, her voice filled with gratitude despite the older woman's harsh words. Salome gave a curt nod, turning away before the emotion in the young mother's eyes could pierce her defenses any further.

As Salome made her way through the village, she passed by clusters of villagers, their voices filled with excitement as they spoke of the star, of the promise of a savior. She caught snippets of their conversation—the hope in their voices, the way they spoke of miracles as though they were real, tangible things. Salome scoffed under her breath, shaking her head as she walked past them, her shoulders hunched against the chill of the evening air.

"A star in the sky," she muttered to herself, her tone dripping with sarcasm. "And suddenly, everyone thinks the world is about to change."

Ahead, she saw an elderly man, Adam, sitting on a low stool, his eyes bright as he spoke to a group of children gathered around him. He was telling them stories—stories of past miracles, of a time when the people had been delivered from their suffering. The children's eyes were wide, their faces filled with wonder, their innocent belief in the coming savior a sharp contrast to Salome's jaded perspective.

She paused, watching them for a moment, her heart clenching at the sight. She had heard those stories once, had believed in them with all her heart. But that was before—before the loss, before the pain that had stripped her of her faith. She turned away, her footsteps quickening as she made her way home, her mind filled with memories she wished she could forget.

The sun was beginning to dip below the horizon, casting long shadows across the village as Salome reached her small home. The streets were quiet, the air heavy with the scent of woodsmoke and the distant cries of children playing. She pushed open the wooden door, the familiar creak filling the silence. The small room was dim, the light from the single oil lamp casting flickering shadows on the walls. Salome set her basket down, her fingers brushing against the worn wood of the table as she let out a heavy sigh. She sank onto the low stool by the fire, her hands resting in her lap, her eyes fixed on the dancing flames.

"A king," she muttered to herself, her voice filled with bitterness. "A savior. What good is a king to people like us? What good is a promise when we have nothing left to give?"

She closed her eyes, the memories flooding her mind—the feel of her child's small hand in hers, the sound of his laughter, the way his eyes had shone with innocence and joy. It had been years, but the pain was still there, a constant ache that refused to fade. She had believed, once. She had prayed, had hoped, had trusted that there was something greater than the suffering they endured. But in the end, all she had been left with was emptiness.

A sudden knock at the door startled her, and Salome's eyes snapped open, her heart pounding. She rose to her feet, her movements slow as she made her way to the door, her hand resting on the latch. She hesitated, her breath catching in her throat. Who could it be at this hour? She took a deep breath, steeling herself before opening the door.

A young man stood on the threshold, his eyes wide, his face flushed with excitement. "Salome," he said, his voice breathless, "you must come. There is a woman—she's in labor, and something is... different. You have to see."

Salome frowned, her brow furrowing as she looked at the young man. "Different? What do you mean?"

He shook his head, his eyes shining with a mixture of fear and awe. "I can't explain it. You just... you have to come."

Salome hesitated, her instincts telling her to stay, to close the door and shut out the world. But there was something in the young man's eyes, something that made her heart clench. She grabbed her basket, her fingers tightening around the handle as she nodded. "Lead the way," she said, her voice brusque, though her heart pounded with a sense of unease.

The young man turned, leading her through the narrow streets, the shadows deepening as the night settled in. Salome followed, her mind racing, her thoughts a jumble of fear and doubt. She had seen enough in her lifetime—enough pain, enough loss, enough disappointment. She had stopped believing in miracles long ago. But as they approached the small house at the edge of the village, she felt a flicker of something deep within her—a whisper, a question, a possibility.

The door was already open, the room beyond filled with the soft glow of candlelight. Salome stepped inside, her eyes immediately drawn to the woman lying on the low bed, her face pale, her breath coming in short, shallow gasps. The air was thick with the scent of sweat and herbs, the tension in the room palpable. A young man knelt by the woman's side, his hand resting on her forehead, his eyes filled with worry.

"Salome," he said, his voice cracking with emotion. "Please. She needs help."

Salome set her basket down, her hands moving with practiced ease as she assessed the situation. The woman's belly was swollen, her skin slick with sweat, her eyes wide with fear. Salome could see the pain etched on her face, the way her body tensed with each contraction. She reached for a cloth, her fingers brushing against the woman's forehead, her voice low and steady as she spoke.

"Breathe, child," she said, her voice surprisingly gentle. "You are strong. You can do this."

The woman's eyes met hers, and for a moment, Salome saw something there—something that made her heart clench. It was hope, fragile and fleeting, but it was there. Salome swallowed, her own emotions threatening to overwhelm her as she continued her work, her hands moving with a precision that came from years of experience.

Hours seemed to pass, the night deepening as the woman labored, her cries filling the small room. Salome remained by her side, her voice a constant presence, her hands steady as she guided the young mother through the pain. She could feel the weight of the room, the way the others watched her, their eyes filled with hope and fear. She had seen this before—had seen the way people looked to her, expecting her to perform miracles she could not promise.

And then, finally, the cry of a newborn pierced the air, a sound so pure, so filled with life, that it took Salome's breath away. She lifted the child, her hands trembling as she looked down at the tiny face, the eyes still closed, the small chest rising and falling with each breath. The room seemed to hold its breath, the silence almost sacred, as if the very air recognized the significance of this moment. Salome felt her heart swell, an emotion she had long buried rising to the surface—something like hope, something like awe. The young mother reached out, her eyes glistening with tears, and Salome gently placed the newborn in her arms. The woman's sobs of joy filled the room, and for a moment, Salome allowed herself to believe that perhaps, just perhaps, there was still light in this world.

CHAPTER 6: HEROD'S SHADOW

"What did you say?" The goblet slipped from King Herod's hand, the wine spilling across the polished marble floor in a dark, spreading stain. He leaned forward on his throne, his eyes narrowing as he fixed his gaze on the trembling advisor before him. The room seemed to hold its breath, the flickering torches casting long shadows across the walls, giving the space a sinister, almost haunted feel.

The advisor swallowed, his face pale, beads of sweat glistening on his brow. "Your Majesty," he stammered, his voice barely audible, "the magi… they have spoken of a star. A sign in the heavens, heralding the birth of a new king. The King of the Jews."

Herod's lips twisted into a sneer, a dark glint in his eyes. "The King of the Jews," he repeated, his voice dripping with disdain. He rose from his throne, his robes rustling, the golden embroidery catching the dim light as he paced the length of the room. His heart pounded, a mix of fear and fury boiling in his chest. The prophecy. He had heard whispers of it before, the rumors of a child who would rise to challenge him, to take what was his.

Herod was known for his ruthlessness, his paranoia—traits that had kept him in power for years, traits that had earned him both fear and hatred. He had crushed dissent without mercy, executed those who dared to question his authority, and even killed members of his own family to maintain his grip on the throne. But beneath the veneer of power, there was fear. A fear that his reign was not as secure as he wanted the world to believe, that something—or someone—could come and take it all away.

"How dare they," he muttered, his hands clenching into fists. "How dare they speak of a king other than me?" He turned sharply, his eyes locking onto the advisor, who shrank back under his gaze. "Where are these magi now?"

The advisor hesitated, his eyes darting to the floor. "They... they are still in Jerusalem, Your Majesty," he said. "They have been seeking information, asking about the child."

Herod's nostrils flared, his jaw tightening. He had worked too hard, sacrificed too much to secure his place on the throne. He would not allow some mythical prophecy to undo everything he had built. His mind raced, a cold determination settling over him. He needed to know more. He needed to find this child before it was too late.

Herod lashed out suddenly, his hand striking the goblet that still lay on the floor, sending it clattering across the room. The advisor flinched, his face paling even more, but he did not move. Herod's eyes blazed, his breath coming in short, angry bursts. He could not—he would not—let this threat go unanswered.

"Bring them to me," Herod ordered, his voice cold and commanding. "I want to speak with these magi myself. I want to know everything they know."

The advisor bowed hastily, backing out of the room, his footsteps echoing down the corridor. Herod stood alone, his eyes narrowing as he stared at the dark stain on the marble floor. The words of the prophecy echoed in his mind—a king who would bring hope to the people, who would challenge his rule. A spark of fear flickered deep within him, but he quickly smothered it, his eyes hardening.

"No one will take my throne," he whispered, his voice filled with venom. "No one."

* * *

Later that evening, Herod sat in his chambers, the curtains drawn tightly, blocking out the night. The room was dimly lit, the flickering flames casting long, shifting shadows on the walls. He could hear the faint sound of music drifting up from the feast below, the laughter of his guests, the clinking of goblets. It all felt hollow, meaningless, against the weight of the news he had just received.

His wife, Herodias, entered the room, her face a mask of concern. She approached him slowly, her fingers brushing against his shoulder as she spoke. "What troubles you, my lord? You left the feast so suddenly."

Herod looked up at her, his eyes filled with a darkness that made her heart clench. "They speak of a new king," he said, his voice low. "A child, born under a star. The magi say he will be the King of the Jews."

Herodias frowned, her eyes narrowing. "A child? What could a child do to threaten you, my king? You have armies, power—"

"It is not just a child," Herod snapped, his voice harsh. "It is the prophecy. The people—they will believe it. They will rally around him, see him as their savior. And if they rise against me, if they dare to challenge my rule…"

Herodias fell silent, her eyes searching his face. She could see the fear there, the anger that simmered just beneath the surface. She knelt beside him, her hands resting on his, her voice softening. "Then find him, my lord," she said. "Find this child and end the threat before it begins."

Herod stared at her, his eyes narrowing. The thought had already crossed his mind, the dark plan forming in the corners of his thoughts. He would not sit idly by while some child grew to challenge him. He would find the child, and he would make sure that the prophecy was never fulfilled.

※ ※ ※

The magi arrived at the palace the next morning, their faces filled with awe and curiosity as they were led through the grand halls, the marble floors gleaming beneath their feet. Herod watched them from his throne, his eyes narrowing as they approached. The opulence of his court—the golden tapestries, the intricate mosaics, the lavish furnishings—was meant to impress, to intimidate. It was a stark contrast to the humble stable where the child they sought was born.

Herod could see the excitement in their eyes, the hope that seemed to radiate from them, and it made his skin crawl. He had spent his life clawing his way to power, and here were these men, speaking of a child who would supposedly inherit what he had fought so hard to claim.

"Welcome," Herod said, his voice smooth, a false smile curving his lips. "I have heard much about your journey. You have come seeking a child, have you not? A king, born under the light of a star."

Balthazar, the eldest of the magi, stepped forward, bowing deeply. "Yes, Your Majesty," he said, his voice filled with reverence. "We have followed the star from the east, and it has led us here. We seek the one who is born King of the Jews, that we may honor him."

Herod's smile tightened, his eyes narrowing. "A noble quest," he said, his voice smooth, though his heart burned with fury. He leaned forward slightly, his eyes fixed on the magi. "I, too, wish to honor this child. When you find him, bring me word, that I too may go and pay homage."

The magi exchanged a glance, their faces lighting up with

gratitude. Herod could see the flicker of relief in their eyes, the way they believed his words. "We are honored by your support, Your Majesty," Melchior said, bowing once more. "We will surely bring you news of the child once we find him."

Herod nodded, his eyes cold as he watched them leave. The moment the doors closed behind them, his smile vanished, replaced by a scowl. He rose from his throne, his hands clenching at his sides. He would let the magi lead him to the child, let them do the work of finding this so-called king. And when they did, he would ensure that the prophecy was ended before it could even begin.

* * *

As night fell, Herod found himself standing on the balcony of his chambers, his eyes fixed on the horizon. The sky was clear, the stars shining brightly above, and there, in the distance, he could see it—the star that had caused all this turmoil. It blazed against the darkness, its light almost mocking him, a reminder of the threat that loomed over him.

His heart pounded, his thoughts racing. He could feel the fear creeping in, the doubt that whispered in the back of his mind. What if the prophecy was true? What if this child was destined to take everything from him? He shook his head, his jaw tightening. No. He would not allow it. He had fought too hard, sacrificed too much to let it all slip away.

He turned, his eyes cold as he looked back at the palace, the grand halls that had been built to honor him, the throne that was his by right. He would do whatever it took to protect what was his. He would not let a mere child take it from him. He would find the child, and he would make sure that the prophecy was nothing more than a forgotten whisper.

A plan began to form in his mind, dark and ruthless. He would not only find the child—he would make sure that no other child could rise to challenge him. He would wipe out any threat, any possibility of this prophecy coming true. His heart hardened, a cold determination settling over him.

"No one will take my throne," he whispered, his voice filled with venom. "No one."

CHAPTER 7: THE CENSUS DECREE

"Joseph, did you hear? We have to go to Bethlehem." Mary's voice was strained, her eyes wide with worry as she leaned against the doorway of their small home. The afternoon sun filtered through the wooden beams, casting a warm glow across the modest room. Joseph looked up from his work, the tools in his hands momentarily forgotten. He could see the unease etched on her face, the way her fingers gripped the edge of her shawl, and his heart sank.

"Bethlehem?" he repeated, his brow furrowing. "Why?"

Mary took a deep breath, her hand moving instinctively to her swollen belly. "The decree from Caesar Augustus," she said. "Everyone must return to their ancestral towns to be registered. Bethlehem is your family's town, Joseph. We must go."

Joseph's heart clenched at her words. The journey to Bethlehem was not a short one—especially not for Mary, who was so far along in her pregnancy. He set down his tools, crossing the room to stand beside her. He placed a gentle hand on her shoulder, his eyes searching hers. "It's not safe for you to travel in your condition," he said, his voice filled with concern. "There must be another way."

Mary shook her head, her eyes filled with determination despite her fear. "We have no choice," she said. "The decree is for everyone. If we do not go, we risk punishment. We must trust in God, Joseph. He will watch over us."

Joseph nodded, though his heart was heavy with worry. He had always been a man of faith, but the thought of taking Mary on such a long journey, with the child so close to being born, filled him with dread. He could see the strain in her eyes, the weariness that had settled over her as the months had passed. But there was no other option. The decree was clear, and they had to obey.

He turned his gaze to the window, the sun beginning to dip below the horizon, casting long shadows across the room. The weight of Roman rule pressed down on them, an ever-present reminder of their powerlessness. He clenched his jaw, a flicker of resentment bubbling beneath his calm exterior. Why now? Why should Mary have to endure this, all because of the whims of a distant ruler? But even as the frustration rose, he took a deep breath, steadying himself. Their faith would guide them, just as it always had.

"Then we will go," he said, his voice steady despite the fear that gnawed at him. He reached for her hand, holding it gently. "We will leave at first light. And I promise you, Mary, I will do everything in my power to keep you safe."

Mary smiled, her eyes softening as she looked at him. "I know you will, Joseph," she said. "And I trust that God will guide us."

※ ※ ※

The morning came too quickly, the first rays of sunlight barely touching the horizon as Joseph and Mary prepared to leave. The air was crisp, a chill lingering in the early dawn that seemed to seep into their bones. Joseph loaded their few belongings onto the back of the donkey, his hands moving with careful precision as he secured the bundles. He glanced over at Mary, who stood by the door, her face pale, her eyes tired. He could see the strain in her posture, the way she leaned slightly against the doorframe, and his heart ached.

"Are you ready?" he asked, his voice gentle.

Mary nodded, though she looked anything but ready. "As ready as I can be," she said, her voice soft. She took a deep breath, her hand resting on her belly. "We must trust in God's plan, Joseph. He has brought us this far, and He will see us through."

Joseph offered her a small smile, though the worry still lingered in his eyes. "Yes," he said, his voice filled with quiet conviction. "We will trust in His plan."

He helped Mary onto the donkey, his hands steady as he guided her. She winced slightly, her face tightening with discomfort, and Joseph felt a pang of guilt. He wished he could spare her this journey, wished there was another way. But he knew that this was something they had to face together, that they had to trust in the path that had been laid before them.

As they set out, the streets of Nazareth were still quiet, the village slowly waking to the new day. The sound of the donkey's hooves echoed softly against the cobblestone, mingling with the distant clatter of pots and the low murmur of voices as people began their morning routines. Joseph walked beside Mary, his hand resting on the donkey's reins, his eyes scanning their surroundings. He could feel the weight of the journey ahead pressing down on him, the uncertainty of what lay before them.

Mary's gaze drifted to the horizon, her eyes clouded with both worry and hope. She reached into the folds of her shawl, pulling out a small wooden carving—an angel, simple and worn from years of being held. It had been a gift from her mother, a symbol of protection and faith. She ran her thumb over its smooth surface, the familiar texture bringing her comfort. She closed her eyes for a moment, whispering a silent prayer, asking for strength, for guidance, for the safety of the child she carried.

Joseph glanced at her, his heart swelling with a mixture of love and admiration. Despite her weariness, despite the fear he knew she must feel, Mary's faith never wavered. She was strong—stronger than anyone he had ever known. He reached out, his hand brushing against hers, and she looked at him, her eyes filled with gratitude.

"We will get through this," he said, his voice barely above a whisper. "Together."

Mary nodded, her eyes glistening with unshed tears. "Together," she echoed, her voice steady despite the emotion that threatened to spill over.

The road ahead was long, the journey fraught with uncertainty. They would have to cross hills and valleys, endure the cold nights and the heat of the day. But as they walked, the starry sky above slowly giving way to the light of dawn, there was a sense of purpose that carried them forward. They were not just obeying a decree—they were part of something greater, something that went beyond their understanding.

Joseph looked up at the sky, the first rays of sunlight breaking through the darkness, and he felt a quiet determination settle over him. No matter the challenges, no matter the hardships, they would see this journey through. They had to. And as they made their way down the dusty path, the distant hills of Bethlehem calling to them, he knew that they were not alone.

In the quiet moments between their steps, as the world around them began to wake, Joseph found himself remembering a dream he had had a few nights ago—a dream of a child, cradled in light, surrounded by warmth and love. He had woken with a sense of peace, a sense that despite the trials they faced, everything would be alright. He hadn't told Mary about it, not yet. But now, as they made their way toward Bethlehem, he felt that same peace settle in his heart once more.

"God is with us," he whispered, his eyes on the horizon. And in that moment, he believed it with all his heart.

CHAPTER 8: THE JOURNEY BEGINS

"I told you they wouldn't make it far." A sharp voice cut through the early morning mist, followed by the faint sound of laughter. Mary lowered her gaze, her fingers gripping the edges of her shawl, her cheeks flushed with a mixture of embarrassment and frustration. She could feel the eyes of the villagers on her and Joseph as they made their way out of Nazareth, whispers trailing them like shadows.

Joseph kept his head high, his jaw clenched, his eyes fixed on the road ahead. He knew what the people thought of them—he had seen the judgment in their eyes, heard the muttered words as they passed by. But he could not let it deter him. He had made a promise to Mary, to protect her and the child she carried, and he would see it through, no matter what anyone else said or thought.

The donkey trudged along, its hooves crunching against the gravel path. Mary swayed gently with its movements, her face pale, her eyes tired. She shifted on the donkey's back, trying to find a more comfortable position, but the strain of the journey was evident in her every movement. Joseph walked beside her, his hand resting on the donkey's bridle, his heart heavy with concern. He knew how difficult this journey would be for Mary, how much it would ask of her, but he also knew that they had no choice. The decree from Caesar Augustus had left them with no other option.

The landscape around them was stark and barren, the sun just beginning to rise over the hills, bathing the world in a soft golden light. The air was cool, the scent of earth and wild herbs filling their senses. Joseph glanced at Mary, his heart aching at the sight of her weariness. Her hands clutched at the donkey's mane, her back hunched slightly as she tried to bear the discomfort. He wished he could do more for her, wished he could ease her burden. But all he could do was be there, to walk beside her, to offer her his strength when she had none left.

"Are you alright?" he asked, his voice gentle, his eyes searching hers.

Mary looked at him, her lips curving into a small, tired smile. "I'm alright," she said, though her voice was strained. "We knew this wouldn't be easy, Joseph. But we have to trust in God's plan. He will see us through."

Joseph nodded, though his heart still ached with worry. He admired Mary's strength, her unwavering faith, even in the face of such hardship. She was stronger than anyone he had ever known, and he loved her all the more for it. He reached for her hand, his fingers brushing against hers, and she squeezed his hand gently, her eyes meeting his.

"We're in this together," she whispered, her voice filled with quiet determination. "No matter what."

Joseph smiled, his heart swelling with love. "Yes," he said. "Together. Always."

* * *

The road was long, winding through the hills and valleys, the sun climbing higher in the sky as the day wore on. The heat grew more intense, the air dry and stifling, and Joseph could see the toll it was taking on Mary. Her face was pale, her breathing shallow, her eyes heavy with exhaustion. He led the donkey off the road, towards a small grove of fig trees, their branches offering some shade from the relentless sun.

"We'll rest here for a while," Joseph said, his voice filled with concern as he helped Mary down from the donkey. She winced, her face tightening with pain, and Joseph's heart clenched. He guided her to a patch of soft grass beneath the trees, his hands gentle as he helped her sit down.

Mary leaned back against the trunk of the tree, her eyes closing, her hand resting on her swollen belly. Joseph knelt beside her, reaching for the waterskin, offering it to her. "Drink," he said, his voice soft. "You need to stay hydrated."

Mary took the waterskin, her hands trembling slightly as she brought it to her lips. She drank slowly, her eyes meeting Joseph's, and she offered him a weak smile. "Thank you," she whispered.

Joseph nodded, his hand resting on her shoulder. He could feel the tension in her body, the strain of the journey weighing heavily on her. He wished he could take away her pain, wished he could make this easier for her. But all he could do was be there, to support her, to protect her as best he could.

"We will rest here for as long as you need," he said, his voice filled with quiet determination.

Mary nodded, her eyes closing once more, her breaths slowing as she leaned back, her body relaxing slightly. Joseph watched her, his heart filled with a mixture of love and worry. He knew how much this journey was asking of her, how much strength it took for her to keep going. And yet, despite it all, she had never once complained, never once wavered in her faith.

The afternoon sun filtered through the branches, casting dappled shadows on the ground. Joseph could hear the distant chirping of birds, the rustle of leaves in the gentle breeze. He kept his senses on high alert, his eyes scanning the horizon. The road was not safe—there were bandits, wild animals, and the ever-present threat of Roman soldiers. He kept his hand on the staff at his side, ready to protect Mary and the child she carried at all costs.

As they rested, Joseph's mind wandered back to a conversation he had overheard in Nazareth before they left—a group of travelers speaking in hushed tones about bandits operating along the roads. The memory made his heart pound, a sense of unease settling over him. He looked at Mary, her face peaceful as she rested, and he knew he had to remain vigilant. He could not afford to let his guard down, not even for a moment.

The sun began to dip below the horizon, the sky painted in hues of orange and pink, and Joseph knew they needed to keep moving. He reached for Mary's hand, his voice gentle as he spoke. "We should go. We need to find a place to rest for the night."

Mary opened her eyes, her face pale, her eyes filled with exhaustion. She nodded, her lips curving into a small, tired smile. "Yes," she said, her voice barely a whisper. "Let's keep going."

Joseph helped her to her feet, his hands steady as he guided her back to the donkey. He could see the strain in her posture, the way her shoulders drooped, the lines of pain etched into her face. He wished he could do more for her, wished he could ease her burden. But all he could do was be there, to walk beside her, to offer her his strength when she had none left.

*　*　*

The night was cool, the stars scattered across the sky like a thousand tiny lanterns. Joseph led the donkey along the winding path, his eyes scanning the landscape, his heart pounding with a mixture of fear and determination. They were far from home, far from any sense of safety, and the road ahead was still uncertain.

Mary was silent, her head resting against the donkey's neck, her eyes closed. Joseph could see the exhaustion in her posture, the way her body swayed with each step. He reached up, his hand resting gently on her knee. "We're almost there," he said, his voice filled with quiet reassurance. "We'll find a place to rest soon."

Mary opened her eyes, her gaze meeting his. She smiled, her eyes filled with love and trust. "I know," she whispered. "I trust you, Joseph. I trust that God will see us through."

Joseph nodded, his heart swelling with love and admiration. She was so strong—stronger than anyone he had ever known. Despite the pain, the fear, the uncertainty, she had never wavered in her faith. And for that, Joseph loved her all the more.

As the night wore on, Joseph spotted a small cave nestled in the hillside, its entrance partially hidden by a cluster of shrubs. He led the donkey towards it, his heart pounding with relief. It wasn't much, but it would provide them with shelter for the night, a place where Mary could rest.

He helped her down from the donkey, his hands gentle as he guided her into the cave. The air inside was cool, the ground covered in soft earth. Joseph laid out a blanket, helping Mary to sit down, her face pale, her breaths coming in shallow gasps.

"Rest, Mary," he said, his voice filled with love. "You need your strength."

Mary nodded, her eyes heavy with exhaustion. She lay back against the blanket, her hand resting on her belly. "God is with us," she whispered, her voice barely audible.

Joseph knelt beside her, his hand resting on her cheek, his heart swelling with emotion. "Yes," he said, his voice thick with emotion. "He is with us. Always."

As the first light of dawn began to break over the horizon, Joseph sat beside Mary, his heart filled with a mixture of fear and hope. The journey had been long, and the road ahead was still uncertain. But in that small cave, beneath the watchful eyes of the stars, Joseph felt a sense of peace. They had each other, and they had their faith. And that, he knew, would be enough to see them through.

And as the sun began to rise, casting its golden light over the hills, Joseph knew that no matter what lay ahead, they would face it together. With faith, with love, and with the knowledge that they were part of something far greater than themselves—a story that was only just beginning.

CHAPTER 9: DANGER ON THE ROAD

"Hold on, Mary!" Joseph shouted, his voice barely audible over the deafening roar of the wind. The atmosphere had shifted in an instant—one moment, the sky was clear and calm, and the next, dark storm clouds rolled in from the west, swallowing the sun. The air thickened with a sense of foreboding, the first gusts of wind tugging at their cloaks, followed by the cold sting of raindrops. In mere moments, the storm was upon them, the rain turning into a torrential downpour, soaking them to the bone.

The donkey brayed in fear, its hooves slipping on the muddy path, and Joseph tightened his grip on the bridle, his heart pounding with a mixture of fear and determination. The road beneath them had turned treacherous, the once-solid ground transforming into a mire of mud and water, making every step a struggle.

Mary clung to the donkey, her face pale, her knuckles white as she held on. The wind whipped her shawl around her, her hair plastered to her face, and she struggled to keep her balance as the donkey stumbled forward. The storm had come out of nowhere, and now they were caught in its fury, the road vanishing in the blinding sheets of rain.

"We have to find shelter!" Joseph called, his voice strained as he looked around, his eyes squinting against the downpour. He shielded Mary with his body, his arm reaching up to steady her as she swayed with each movement of the frightened animal. He could feel the fear gnawing at him—the fear that he might not be able to keep her safe, that the storm would overwhelm them before they could find refuge.

A flash of lightning illuminated the landscape for a brief moment, and Joseph spotted the outline of a structure in the distance—a small building, its roof barely visible through the storm. "There!" he shouted, pointing towards it. "We have to make it to that shelter!"

Mary nodded, her eyes filled with a mixture of fear and trust. She held on as Joseph led the donkey forward, his feet sinking into the mud with every step, the rain stinging his skin. The wind howled around them, the sky flashing with bursts of lightning, the thunder rumbling like a warning from the heavens. Each step was a battle, Joseph's muscles aching as he fought against the storm, his only thought to get Mary to safety.

Finally, they reached the building—a small, dilapidated hut, its roof sagging, the walls made of rough-hewn stone. Joseph pushed open the door, the wood creaking beneath his weight, and led Mary inside, the donkey following close behind. The air inside was damp, the scent of mildew and earth filling their senses, but it was shelter—protection from the storm that raged outside.

Mary sank to the ground, her breaths coming in shallow gasps, her face pale with exhaustion. Joseph knelt beside her, his hand resting gently on her shoulder. "Are you alright?" he asked, his voice filled with concern, his eyes searching hers.

Mary nodded, though her eyes were filled with weariness. "I'm alright," she said, her voice barely a whisper. "Just... tired."

Joseph reached for the waterskin, offering it to her. "Drink," he said, his voice soft. "You need your strength."

Mary took the waterskin, her hands trembling as she brought it to her lips. She drank slowly, her eyes meeting Joseph's, and she offered him a weak smile. "Thank you," she whispered.

Joseph smiled, though his heart was heavy with worry. He could see the toll the journey was taking on her, the strain of the storm, the exhaustion etched into her features. He wished he could do more, wished he could take away her pain, but all he could do was be there, to support her, to protect her as best he could.

The door to the hut suddenly creaked open, and Joseph's heart lurched, his hand instinctively reaching for the staff at his side. A figure stepped inside, the rain streaming off his cloak, his face partially obscured by the hood. Joseph rose to his feet, his body tensed, his eyes narrowing as he faced the stranger.

The man pulled back his hood, revealing a weathered face, his eyes sharp, his expression guarded. He was dressed in the armor of a Roman centurion, the insignia on his cloak marking him as a soldier of rank. Cassius had served in the Roman army for nearly two decades, climbing the ranks through a combination of skill and sheer determination. He had seen the brutality of the empire firsthand, witnessed the oppression of the people, and had long since stopped believing in the righteousness of Rome. Yet, duty held him—duty to his men, to the structure of the life he had known for so long. But now, in moments like this, he found himself questioning what all of it was for. Joseph's heart pounded, his grip tightening on the staff, his mind racing. A Roman soldier—what did he want? What was he doing here?

The man raised a hand, his voice calm despite the storm raging outside. "Peace," he said, his eyes meeting Joseph's. "I mean you no harm. I saw you struggling on the road. I came to offer shelter." As he spoke, there was a hesitation in his tone—a vulnerability that hinted at a weariness not just from the storm, but from a life spent serving a cause he no longer believed in. Cassius had grown tired of the empire's endless demands, the way they crushed those beneath their heel without a second thought. He had followed orders without question for so long, but the faces of those he had harmed haunted him in the quiet moments between battles.

Joseph hesitated, his eyes flickering to Mary, who watched the exchange with wide, wary eyes. He could see the exhaustion in her face, the way her body trembled with fatigue, and he knew they couldn't afford to turn away help—not now, not in this storm.

"Thank you," Joseph said, his voice cautious, his eyes never leaving the centurion's. "We are grateful for any assistance."

The man nodded, stepping further into the hut, his eyes scanning the small, dim space. He removed his cloak, shaking off the rain, and hung it on a hook near the door. "My name is Cassius," he said, his voice steady. "I am stationed nearby, but the storm has made travel impossible. I saw you on the road and thought it best to help."

Joseph nodded, though his heart still pounded with a mixture of fear and distrust. The Romans were not known for their kindness—especially not towards the people of Judea. But there was something in Cassius's eyes, something that spoke of sincerity, of a desire to help, and Joseph knew they had no choice but to trust him, at least for the moment.

"This is my wife, Mary," Joseph said, his voice filled with quiet strength. "She is with child, and we are on our way to Bethlehem. The storm caught us by surprise."

Cassius's gaze softened as he looked at Mary, who offered him a small, tired smile. "You are brave to travel in such conditions," he said, his voice filled with a mixture of admiration and concern. "The roads are treacherous, and the storm is unforgiving. But you are safe here, for now."

Joseph nodded, his heart swelling with gratitude despite his lingering distrust. "Thank you," he said, his voice sincere. "Your kindness is appreciated."

Cassius offered a small smile, his eyes meeting Joseph's. "It is not kindness, merely duty," he said, his voice soft. "We are all human, after all. And in times like these, we must help one another." He paused, his gaze dropping for a moment as if considering his next words. "In truth, I am weary of what my duty has become. Rome speaks of order, of strength, but all I have seen is suffering. The people we subjugate, the lives we take… sometimes I wonder if there is any justice left in the world."

The words hung in the air, a reminder of the shared humanity that transcended the divisions of empire and power. Joseph felt a pang of something deep within him—something like hope, something like the faint glimmer of understanding. He nodded, his eyes meeting Cassius's, and for a moment, the tension seemed to ease, the storm outside a distant roar.

The night wore on, the storm raging outside, the wind howling, the rain pounding against the walls of the hut. Cassius sat by the door, his eyes scanning the darkness, his posture relaxed but alert. Joseph sat beside Mary, his hand resting on hers, his heart filled with a mixture of fear and gratitude. The journey had been long, and the road ahead was still uncertain, but for now, they were safe, sheltered from the storm, and that was enough.

Mary leaned against Joseph, her eyes heavy with exhaustion, her breaths slow and steady. Joseph watched her, his heart swelling with love and admiration. She was so strong—stronger than anyone he had ever known. Despite the pain, the fear, the uncertainty, she had never once wavered in her faith. And for that, Joseph loved her all the more.

Cassius glanced over at them, his eyes softening as he watched the young couple. "You must have great faith," he said, his voice barely audible over the sound of the storm. "To endure so much, to keep going despite everything." He hesitated, then continued, his voice filled with a hint of longing. "I envy that. I have followed Rome's orders my entire life, and yet I have never felt such certainty, such peace. Watching you both… it makes me wonder if there is something I have missed—something greater than all of this."

Joseph looked up, his eyes meeting Cassius's. He nodded, his voice filled with quiet conviction. "We do," he said. "We trust in God's plan, even when it seems impossible. He has brought us this far, and He will see us through."

Cassius was silent for a moment, his eyes thoughtful. He looked away, his gaze fixed on the darkness beyond the door. "Faith," he murmured, his voice filled with a mixture of wonder and longing. "It is a powerful thing. I have seen it move mountains, and yet, I have never been able to grasp it myself."

Joseph watched him, his heart aching with a mixture of empathy and understanding. He could see the struggle in Cassius's eyes, the uncertainty that lay beneath the surface. He knew what it was to doubt, to question, to wonder if there was truly something greater than themselves. But he also knew the power of faith, the strength it gave them, the hope that carried them through even the darkest of times.

"Perhaps," Joseph said, his voice gentle, "faith is not something to grasp, but something to be given. A gift, not a possession."

Cassius looked at him, his eyes filled with a mixture of curiosity and longing. He nodded slowly, his gaze drifting back to the storm outside. "Perhaps," he said, his voice barely audible. "Perhaps you are right. Perhaps there is more to this world than orders and power. Perhaps there is a light, even in the darkest places." He paused, his expression pensive. "Maybe it's time I started looking for it."

The storm began to ease, the wind dying down, the rain slowing to a gentle patter against the roof. The first light of dawn began to break over the horizon, the sky painted in soft hues of pink and gold. Cassius looked towards the faint glow, his expression contemplative. "It seems the storm is finally passing," he said quietly.

Joseph nodded, his eyes following the light. "A new day," he whispered, a sense of hope washing over him. He turned to Mary, brushing a strand of hair from her face. "We should prepare to leave soon, once you're ready."

Mary smiled weakly, her eyes filled with determination despite her weariness. "Yes," she said, her voice steady. "We must keep moving."

Cassius stood, his movements slow, his eyes lingering on the young couple. "May your journey be blessed," he said, his voice filled with a sincerity that caught Joseph by surprise. "I will not forget this night, nor the faith you have shown."

Joseph extended his hand, and Cassius took it, their eyes meeting in a moment of silent understanding. "Thank you, Cassius," Joseph said. "For everything."

Cassius nodded, a faint smile touching his lips. "Go in peace," he said. And with that, he turned, slipping out of the hut and disappearing into the early morning mist, leaving Mary and Joseph to continue their journey, the first rays of sunlight guiding their way.

CHAPTER 10: ELI'S REVELATION

Eli squinted up at the night sky, his breath misting in the cold air. His heart began to race, and he felt an inexplicable tension settle over him. The cold air seemed to thicken, and his hands started to tremble slightly as if his body knew something extraordinary was about to happen. The other shepherds murmured quietly around the fire, their voices a low hum against the backdrop of the distant bleating of sheep. He had always loved these quiet nights out in the fields—nights where the worries of the world seemed to drift away with the smoke, leaving only the comforting rhythm of the stars and the warmth of the fire. But tonight, something was different.

The sky seemed brighter, the stars more vivid than usual, as if the heavens themselves were trying to tell him something. The sudden shift in the atmosphere made Eli's skin prickle, a strange sensation of both anticipation and fear building inside him. He shifted, his eyes scanning the horizon, and that was when he saw it—a star unlike any he had ever seen before. It was larger, brighter, and it seemed to pulse with a light so intense that it took his breath away. Eli's pulse quickened, and his instinctive urge was to both flee and stay rooted in awe. He could feel his heart pounding, and a deep sense of reverence washed over him.

"Eli, what's caught your eye?" a voice called from the fire. It was

Nathan, one of the older shepherds, his voice roughened by years of shouting commands to stubborn sheep. He stood, his eyes narrowing as he followed Eli's gaze.

"Look at that," Eli said, his voice barely more than a whisper, filled with awe. He pointed up to the sky, his arm trembling slightly. Nathan's eyes widened as he spotted the star, his face softening with wonder.

"By the Almighty," Nathan murmured, his voice filled with reverence. "I've never seen anything like it."

The other shepherds gathered around, their faces turned upward, their eyes wide with awe. Some of them fell to their knees, unable to stand beneath the brilliance of the light, while others shielded their eyes, their hands trembling. The air felt charged, almost electric, and Eli could see the fear and amazement etched into each of their expressions. The star seemed to glow brighter, its light casting an overwhelming radiance across the fields, illuminating the shepherds with a glow so powerful that Eli felt tears spring to his eyes. His heart swelled with something beyond words—a mixture of awe, fear, and an unexpected, fragile hope. It was more than awe, more than wonder—it was hope, fragile and fleeting, yet powerful enough to bring tears to his eyes.

"Do you think..." Eli hesitated, his voice catching in his throat. He looked at Nathan, his eyes searching the older man's face. "Do you think it could mean something? A sign, perhaps?"

Nathan was silent for a moment, his eyes still fixed on the star. He took a deep breath, his voice low as he spoke. "I don't know, Eli," he said. "But I've heard the stories, the prophecies. A child who would bring justice, who would save us from this world of cruelty and suffering." He looked at Eli, his eyes filled with a mixture of hope and fear. "Maybe... maybe this is the sign we've been waiting for."

Eli's heart pounded, his breath catching in his chest. The prophecies—he had heard them all his life, stories whispered by the elders, tales of a Messiah who would bring peace, who would lift the burdens of the people, who would make right all the injustices they had endured. Yet, Eli had always struggled to believe them, thinking they were just tales to comfort the oppressed. But now, beneath the light of the star, those doubts seemed to crumble, replaced by a stirring deep within him, a flicker of belief that perhaps the stories were more than just tales. But those had always been just that—stories, tales told to comfort children, to give hope in the face of hardship. And yet, as he looked up at the star, he felt something stir deep within him, a flicker of belief that maybe, just maybe, those stories were more than just tales.

The other shepherds were silent, their eyes fixed on the sky, their faces filled with the same awe and hope that Eli felt. He could see the internal struggle in some of them—simple men grappling with the enormity of what they were witnessing. A few looked unsure, as if questioning why they, of all people, had been chosen to witness something so divine. He could see it in their eyes—the longing, the desire for something greater, for a light that could cut through the darkness of their lives. They were simple men, men who spent their days in the fields, who knew the harshness of life, the cruelty of the world. But in that moment, beneath the light of the star, they were united by something greater, something that transcended the hardships they faced.

"Maybe it's a sign," Eli said, his voice filled with quiet conviction. "Maybe it's telling us that something is coming. That hope is still possible, even for men like us, shepherds with nothing to offer but our faith."

Nathan nodded, his eyes shining with tears. "Hope," he repeated, his voice barely more than a whisper. "Maybe that's what we need. Maybe that's what this is all about."

Eli looked up at the star, his heart pounding with a mixture of fear and hope. He didn't know what the future held, didn't know if the star truly was a sign of something greater. But he knew one thing—he couldn't ignore the feeling deep within him, the sense that something was about to change, that the world was on the brink of something extraordinary.

The fire crackled softly, the sheep bleating in the distance, and Eli closed his eyes, taking a deep breath. He could feel the warmth of the fire on his skin, the cool night air filling his lungs, and the light of the star washing over him, filling him with a sense of peace he hadn't felt in years. It was as if the world had paused, just for a moment, to give them this—this glimpse of something greater, this hope that maybe, just maybe, the stories were true.

"Eli," Nathan said, his voice breaking the silence. Eli opened his eyes, looking at the older man. Nathan's face was solemn, his eyes filled with determination. "We have to share this. We have to tell the others. If this is truly a sign, if the Messiah has come… we can't keep this to ourselves."

Eli nodded, his heart swelling with determination. "You're right," he said, his voice steady. "We can't keep this to ourselves. If this is truly the sign we've been waiting for, then we have to share the hope we've been given—no matter who we are or what doubts we may have."

Nathan smiled, his eyes softening. "Then let's go," he said. "The night is still young, and there are many who need to hear this."

Eli turned, his eyes lingering on the star for a moment longer before he nodded, his heart pounding with a mixture of fear and excitement. He could feel the weight of the moment, the sense that they were part of something far greater than themselves. And as he turned to follow Nathan, to share the hope they had found, he knew that this was just the beginning—that the world was about to change, and that they had a part to play in it.

✽ ✽ ✽

The village was quiet, the only sound the soft rustling of the wind through the trees and the distant bleating of sheep. Eli and Nathan moved quickly, their footsteps barely audible on the dirt path, the cold night air biting at their skin. Their hearts pounded not only from the exertion but also from the weight of what they were about to share—a message so profound that it felt as if it could change everything. They had to share the news, had to tell the others about the star, about the hope they had found.

They reached the edge of the village, the small homes dark, the windows shuttered against the cold night air. Nathan knocked on the door of the first house, his hand firm, his face filled with determination. The door creaked open, a face appearing in the dim light, eyes squinting in confusion.

"Nathan? Eli? What are you doing here at this hour?" The voice was rough with sleep, the man's face lined with weariness.

"We have something to tell you," Nathan said, his voice filled with urgency. "Something important. A sign—a star unlike any we've ever seen. We believe... we believe it could be the sign of the Messiah."

The man's eyes widened, his face softening with a mixture of surprise and wonder. "The Messiah? Are you sure?"

Eli stepped forward, his eyes filled with conviction. "We don't know for sure," he said, his voice steady. "But we saw the star, and we felt something—something that we can't ignore. We believe that hope is coming, that something is about to change."

The man was silent for a moment, his eyes searching Eli's face. Then he nodded, his lips curving into a small, hopeful smile. "Wait here," he said. "I'll wake my family. They need to hear this."

Nathan and Eli nodded, their hearts pounding with a mixture of fear and excitement as they watched the man disappear into the house. They could hear the soft murmur of voices, the rustle of movement, and a moment later, the door opened wider, the man's family stepping out, their faces filled with a mixture of curiosity and hope.

"Tell us," the man said, his voice filled with quiet reverence. "Tell us about the star."

Eli took a deep breath, his eyes shining with determination. He could feel the weight of the moment, the sense that they were part of something far greater than themselves. And as he began to speak, to share the hope they had found, he knew that this was just the beginning—that the world was on the brink of something extraordinary, and that they had a part to play in it.

"We saw a star—a light unlike anything we've ever seen," Eli began, his voice filled with both awe and conviction. "It was brighter, larger, as if it were calling out to us. We believe it could be the sign of the Messiah—the one who will bring justice, who will bring light to our world, who will give hope to the weary and oppressed. It filled us with a sense that everything could be different, that a new beginning was on the horizon.""

The family listened, their faces softening, their eyes shining with a mixture of awe and hope. Eli could see the longing in their eyes, the desire for something greater, for a light that could cut through the darkness of their lives. And as he spoke, he felt a sense of peace wash over him, a sense of purpose that he had never felt before.

"We don't know what the future holds," Eli continued, his voice unwavering. "But we believe this is a sign—a sign that hope is still possible, that justice is coming. We are just shepherds, and we may not understand everything, but we felt called to share this light, to remind everyone that even in darkness, there is hope." And we wanted to share that hope with you."

The man's wife stepped forward, her eyes filled with tears. She reached out, her hand resting gently on Eli's arm. "Thank you," she whispered, her voice thick with emotion. "Thank you for sharing this with us. We need hope now more than ever."

Eli nodded, his heart swelling with emotion. The sight of this small family, their faces lighting up with hope, made him realize just how important it was to share what they had witnessed. The Messiah, if he truly had come, was for everyone—for the powerful and the powerless alike. And as he looked at the family before him, he knew they were part of something that would change the world, that they had a role to play in spreading this hope to everyone they could reach.

The night was still young, the stars shining brightly above, and Eli knew that there were many more who needed to hear the news, who needed to be reminded that hope was still possible. He turned to Nathan, his eyes filled with determination, and nodded.

"Let's keep going," he said, his voice filled with quiet conviction. "There are more who need to hear this."

Nathan smiled, his eyes shining with tears. "Yes," he said. "Let's keep going."

And as they turned to leave, to share the hope they had found, Eli knew that this was just the beginning—that the world was on the brink of something extraordinary, and that they had a part to play in it. They were simple shepherds, men who knew the harshness of life, but in that moment, beneath the light of the star, they were filled with a sense of purpose, a sense of hope that would carry them through whatever lay ahead.

CHAPTER 11: THE MAGI'S TEST

"Get down!" Azar's voice was a desperate whisper, barely audible over the pounding of his own heart. The night was dark, the moon hidden behind a thick blanket of clouds, and the desert lay like an endless ocean of shadows around them. The cold sand beneath their feet seemed to stretch forever, the biting wind sending shivers down their spines. The flickering light of their campfire cast long, dancing shapes across the sand, and in those shapes, Azar had seen movement—uninvited guests, creeping towards them with silent intent.

Gaspar, one of Azar's companions, turned quickly, his eyes widening as he caught sight of the figures approaching. He grabbed his staff, his knuckles turning white as he held it tightly, his gaze locking with Azar's. "Thieves," he hissed, his voice barely audible. "They're coming for us."

Azar's heart pounded, fear clawing at his chest, his hands trembling slightly as adrenaline surged through his veins. He could feel the cold sweat on his brow, his body tensing as his senses heightened, each shadow seeming to move with intent. He had known this journey would not be without danger—traveling through the desert, carrying gold and precious gifts, they were a target for anyone desperate enough to ambush them. But knowing the risk did not make it any easier to face the reality of it.

He looked over at Balthazar, the eldest of their group, who had risen to his feet, his face calm despite the threat that loomed over them. Balthazar's eyes met Azar's, and he nodded, a silent reassurance that steadied Azar's nerves, if only slightly.

"Stay close to the camels," Balthazar said, his voice low but commanding. "Protect the gifts, but more importantly, protect each other. We must not let fear overcome us."

Azar nodded, his throat tight. He moved closer to the camels, his eyes scanning the darkness, his ears straining to catch any sound—footsteps, whispers, the rustle of fabric. The desert was silent, the air thick with tension, and Azar felt a chill run down his spine. He had always believed in the importance of their journey, had trusted that the star would lead them to something extraordinary. But now, in the face of danger, he couldn't help but wonder if it was worth it. Was this truly the path they were meant to take, or had they been foolish to think they could make such a journey without facing the harshness of the world?

Suddenly, a shout broke the silence, followed by the clash of metal—a thief had lunged towards Gaspar, his blade catching the flickering light of the campfire. The sound of steel meeting wood echoed through the night, a harsh reminder of the reality they faced. Gaspar's face twisted in concentration, his breaths coming in quick bursts as he fought to hold his ground. Gaspar parried the blow with his staff, his face twisted in concentration as he fought to hold his ground. Azar's heart lurched, fear gripping him as he watched the struggle. His instincts screamed at him to run, to protect himself, but another part of him, a deeper part, told him he could not abandon his friends. His legs felt like they were made of lead, the weight of fear rooting him to the spot. He wanted to help, to rush forward and defend his friend, but his feet felt like they were rooted to the ground, his body frozen by the terror that coursed through him.

"Azar!" Balthazar's voice cut through the chaos, sharp and

commanding. "Focus! We need you!"

Azar blinked, his gaze snapping to Balthazar, who was fending off another attacker, his staff moving with practiced precision. The fear that had paralyzed Azar seemed to loosen its grip, and he took a deep breath, his hands tightening around his own staff. He couldn't let his friends face this alone. He had to be strong, had to trust that they were on the right path.

With a shout, Azar rushed forward, his staff swinging towards one of the thieves. The man turned, his eyes widening in surprise, and Azar felt a surge of adrenaline as his staff connected with the thief's arm, knocking him off balance. The thief stumbled, falling to the ground, and Azar stood over him, his heart pounding, his breath coming in ragged gasps.

The camp was a blur of movement, the shadows flickering wildly as the firelight danced across the scene. The air was thick with the smell of smoke and sweat, the grunts of exertion and the clash of weapons filling Azar's ears. He could feel the cold sand beneath his feet as he rushed forward, the weight of his staff solid in his hands. Gaspar had managed to disarm his attacker, his staff held high as he stepped forward, his face filled with determination. Balthazar moved with a calm precision, his eyes focused, his movements fluid as he defended himself and the others. And Azar felt a strange sense of clarity wash over him, a realization that this was indeed part of their journey—a test of their resolve and commitment. The fear that had once paralyzed him gave way to determination, a sense that they were being forged through these trials, each challenge strengthening their faith and their bond.

The thieves, realizing they were outmatched, began to retreat, their figures disappearing into the darkness, swallowed by the night. The tension in the camp began to ebb, replaced by an eerie silence, the desert once more settling into a stillness that seemed almost surreal after the chaos. Azar stood still, his chest heaving, his eyes scanning the shadows until he was sure they were gone. The camp fell silent once more, the only sound the crackling of the fire, the distant rustle of the wind across the sand.

Balthazar approached Azar, his hand resting gently on the younger man's shoulder. His own breaths were heavy, but his eyes shone with an unshakable conviction, a steady reassurance that seemed to anchor Azar amidst the chaos. "You did well," he said, his voice filled with warmth. "You faced your fear, and you protected your friends. That is all we can ask of one another."

Azar looked at Balthazar, his heart still pounding, his mind racing. He wanted to believe that they were on the right path, that this journey was worth the danger, but doubt still gnawed at him, a persistent whisper in the back of his mind. "Is it worth it?" he asked, his voice barely audible. "All of this—the danger, the fear—is it truly worth it?"

Balthazar's eyes softened, his gaze filled with understanding. He could see the doubt in Azar's eyes, the weight of the question that hung between them. This journey was not just about following a star—it was about facing the darkness within and without, about choosing faith even when the path seemed uncertain. He nodded, his hand squeezing Azar's shoulder. "It is worth it," he said, his voice steady. "We are following a star, a sign that something extraordinary is happening. The journey is not without its trials, but those trials are what make the destination meaningful. We must have faith, even when it is difficult. Especially when it is difficult."

Azar took a deep breath, his eyes drifting to the sky, to the star that still shone brightly above them, its light a beacon in the darkness. He could feel the weight of Balthazar's words, the truth in them. The journey was not easy, and it was filled with danger, but it was also filled with purpose, with the hope that they were part of something greater than themselves.

Gaspar joined them, his face flushed, his breath coming in heavy gasps. He looked at Azar, a smile tugging at his lips. "We made it," he said, his voice filled with a mixture of relief and triumph. "We faced them, and we made it," Gaspar said, his voice trembling slightly as the adrenaline began to fade. He looked at Azar, his eyes reflecting both relief and a newfound determination. "I was scared, but I think... I think this is what we are meant to do."

Azar nodded, a small smile forming on his own lips. "Yes," he said, his voice steady. "We made it."

Balthazar smiled, his eyes shining with pride. "And we will continue," he said. "We will follow the star, and we will see where it leads us. Together."

Azar looked at his companions, his heart swelling with a mixture of fear and hope. He could see the weariness in their eyes, but also the strength—the belief that what they were doing mattered, that their journey was part of something far greater than themselves. The ambush had tested them, had forced them to confront their fears, but it had also shown them what they were capable of. The journey was far from over, and the road ahead was still uncertain. But he knew that he was not alone, that he had friends who would stand by his side, no matter what. And as he looked up at the star, its light shining brightly in the dark sky, he felt a sense of peace wash over him, a sense of purpose that gave him the strength to keep going.

"Let's rest," Balthazar said, his voice gentle. "We have a long journey ahead of us, and we will need our strength."

The three men moved back towards the campfire, their bodies weary but their hearts filled with a renewed sense of determination. Azar sat down, his eyes still fixed on the star, its light a reminder of why they were on this journey, of the hope that lay ahead. He knew that there would be more challenges, more moments of doubt and fear, but he also knew that they were on the right path, that they were part of something greater than themselves.

And as the fire crackled softly, the desert around them quiet once more, Azar closed his eyes, a sense of calm settling over him. The journey was worth it. The danger, the fear, the trials—they were all part of something beautiful, something extraordinary. This was a journey of faith, of light overcoming darkness, and each test they faced brought them closer to that light. The ambush was not just a threat—it was a reminder that the path to hope was not without obstacles, that they had to fight for the light they sought. And he would see it through, no matter what.

The night stretched on, the stars shining brightly above, and Azar knew that they were not alone—that the light of the star would guide them, that their faith would carry them through whatever lay ahead. And as he drifted off to sleep, his heart filled with hope, he knew that this was just the beginning—that the journey was far from over, and that the best was yet to come. They had faced darkness, but they had also seen the power of standing together, of choosing faith in the face of fear. The star still shone brightly above them, and Azar knew they were being guided—each step, each trial bringing them closer to something extraordinary.

CHAPTER 11: THE STRANGER'S GIFT

"Please, take it," the old man insisted, his voice barely louder than a whisper, yet full of warmth. His clothes were worn, patched in several places, and his hands were calloused, yet his eyes shone with a kindness that seemed to transcend the hardships he had faced. He held out a simple, tattered blanket, its edges frayed, the fabric worn thin from years of use. The old man's hands trembled slightly as he offered it, but there was a gentleness in his gesture that spoke of a genuine desire to help. Mary looked at the blanket, then at the man, her eyes widening with a mixture of surprise and gratitude. She hesitated for a moment, unsure if they could accept such a gift from someone who clearly had so little to give.

They had stopped at a small village on the outskirts of Bethlehem, hoping to find a moment's rest before continuing their journey. The village was a humble place, the homes made of sunbaked bricks, the streets narrow and winding. The people here were poor, their clothes simple, their eyes weary. And yet, in the midst of their struggles, they still found it in their hearts to show kindness to strangers.

Mary glanced at Joseph, who stood beside her, his expression softening as he met the old man's gaze. Joseph could see the sincerity in the man's eyes, a reflection of the hardships he too had faced, yet still, he was willing to give. He nodded gently, his eyes filled with gratitude. He nodded, his eyes filled with gratitude. "Thank you," he said, his voice sincere. "We will take it, and we will cherish it."

The old man smiled, his face crinkling with deep lines, his eyes twinkling beneath the weight of his years. "You remind me of myself, many years ago," he said softly. "My wife and I traveled a long road too, with nothing but hope to keep us warm. It was not an easy journey, but we found kindness along the way, and now, I wish to share a little of that with you." He placed the blanket in Mary's hands, his fingers brushing against hers, and Mary felt a warmth spread through her chest, a sense of comfort that seemed to wrap around her like the very fabric she held.

"It's not much," the old man said, his voice filled with humility. "But it has kept me warm for many years. I have no riches to give, but perhaps this blanket can offer you some comfort on your journey. May it bring warmth to you and your child.""

Mary looked down at the blanket, her fingers brushing against the soft fabric. She could feel the old man's compassion in every stitch, the care that had gone into preserving this simple piece of cloth. It was not just a blanket—it was a piece of his life, a testament to his own struggles and his triumphs over them. She could feel the history in it, the years of use, the care that had gone into keeping it clean and mended. It was a simple thing, and yet it was filled with meaning, with love. She looked up at the old man, her eyes shining with tears. "Thank you," she whispered, her voice thick with emotion. "This means more to me than you could ever know. It gives me hope—hope that we are not alone, that there is still kindness in the world.""

The old man smiled, his eyes softening. "May your journey be blessed," he said, his voice filled with quiet reverence. "And may your child be a light to the world—a beacon of hope, just as you have brought hope to me by accepting this gift.""

Mary nodded, her heart swelling with gratitude. She watched as the old man turned and walked away, his figure disappearing into the narrow streets of the village, his gait slow but steady. She could feel tears welling up in her eyes as she realized how much this simple act of kindness meant—not just the blanket, but the reminder that even in the hardest times, they were not alone. She clutched the blanket to her chest, her eyes closing for a moment as she took a deep breath, the weight of the journey suddenly feeling a little lighter.

Joseph stepped closer, his hand resting gently on her shoulder. "Are you alright?" he asked, his voice filled with concern. He could see the emotion in her eyes, the way the old man's gift had touched her deeply.

Mary opened her eyes, looking up at him, her lips curving into a soft smile. "I'm alright," she said, her voice barely a whisper. "That man... he was so kind. At first, I wasn't sure we should accept it. He seemed to have so little, but the way he spoke, the warmth in his eyes... It makes me feel like we are not alone in this. Like there are still people who care, even in the midst of all this hardship.""

Joseph nodded, his eyes filled with understanding. "It's the small acts of kindness that remind us of the goodness in the world," he said, his voice gentle. "Even when everything else seems uncertain, even when the road ahead is difficult, those moments of compassion give us hope. That blanket is more than just warmth—it's a reminder that we are not walking this journey alone.""

Mary looked down at the blanket, her fingers brushing against the fabric once more. She could feel the warmth of the old man's kindness in every stitch, could feel the love and care that had gone into this simple gift. It was as if the blanket itself was a shield against the coldness of the world—a symbol of the kindness that still existed, even when times were dark. She knew that it was more than just a blanket—it was a symbol of hope, of the belief that even in the darkest of times, there were still people who cared, who were willing to help others.

"We should keep moving," Joseph said, his voice gentle, his eyes filled with concern as he looked at Mary. "Bethlehem is not far now, and we need to find a place to stay before nightfall. I have faith that we will find shelter, just as we have found kindness along the way."

Mary nodded, her heart swelling with determination. She knew that the journey was far from over, that the challenges they faced were still ahead of them. But she also knew that they were not alone. They had each other, and they had the kindness of strangers, the small moments of compassion that made the journey a little easier, a little more bearable.

* * *

The sun was beginning to set as they approached Bethlehem, the sky painted in hues of orange and pink, the first stars just beginning to appear. The streets were bustling with people, travelers who had come for the census, their faces filled with exhaustion, their voices blending together in a cacophony of sound. Joseph led the donkey carefully through the crowd, his eyes scanning the buildings, searching for a place to stay.

Mary held the blanket close, her heart pounding with a mixture of hope and fear. She could feel the exhaustion in her body, the weight of the journey pressing down on her, but she also felt a sense of determination, a sense of purpose that kept her going. She knew that they had to find a place to rest, that the time was drawing near for her child to be born.

CHAPTER 12: THE ARRIVAL IN BETHLEHEM

"**K**eep moving, Mary," Joseph urged gently, his voice thick with exhaustion and worry, his eyes constantly scanning for any sign of shelter. His arm supported Mary as she leaned on him, her steps slow and laborious. The streets of Bethlehem were crowded with people, the air filled with the sound of chatter, the braying of donkeys, and the clatter of carts over cobblestone. The scent of smoke from nearby fires mixed with the earthy smell of animals, while the sights of travelers in worn clothes, children crying, and merchants shouting added to the chaos around them. It was a chaotic scene, and Joseph's heart ached with worry as he watched Mary struggle to keep her footing. The journey had been long and grueling, and now, as they stood at the gates of the city, their greatest challenge lay before them: finding a place to rest.

Mary nodded, her face pale, her eyes filled with determination despite the pain coursing through her. She could feel each step radiate discomfort through her body, the weight of the baby pressing heavily against her as if testing her resolve. Her breaths came in short gasps, her mind flickering between hope and the fear that they might not find a place in time. She clutched her swollen belly, her breaths coming in short, shallow gasps. The baby was close—she could feel it. Each step seemed to send a jolt of pain through her body, but she pressed on, her gaze fixed ahead, her heart filled with hope. They had come so far, had endured so much, and now they were here. There had to be a place for them, a corner where they could rest, where their child could be born.

Joseph scanned the bustling streets, his eyes darting from one inn to the next, his heart tightening each time they were met with rejection. He could feel a growing sense of desperation gnawing at him—he was torn between his concern for Mary and the pressing need to find shelter. Every closed door felt like another failure, a promise left unfulfilled. Each door they approached was met with rejection—a shake of the head, a hurried apology, or sometimes even a dismissive wave as innkeepers turned back to their own concerns. Most of them were too preoccupied with their own guests, overwhelmed by the influx of travelers. A few showed a flicker of sympathy when they saw Mary, but even then, they could offer no help. The city was overflowing with travelers, all here for the census, and there was no room, no space for a young couple in need.

"Please," Joseph said, his voice cracking as he spoke to yet another innkeeper, his hands clasped in desperation. "My wife is with child. We just need a small space, somewhere for her to rest."

The innkeeper's eyes softened as he looked at Mary, his expression filled with regret. He sighed, a weariness in his eyes that hinted at the stress of the crowded city, but also a genuine sadness that he could not help them. He shook his head, his voice apologetic. "I'm sorry, friend. There is no room here. Every bed is taken."

Joseph's shoulders slumped, his heart sinking further into despair. He could feel the weight of his failure, the promise to protect her slipping further from his grasp with each rejection. He looked at Mary, her face flushed, her eyes filled with exhaustion, and he felt a wave of helplessness wash over him. He had promised to protect her, to keep her safe, and now, when she needed him most, he felt as if he were failing her.

Mary reached out, her hand resting on his arm, her touch gentle and reassuring. Despite her exhaustion, she could see the pain in Joseph's eyes—the way his sense of responsibility weighed heavily on him. She offered him a small smile, a reminder that they were in this together. "We will find a place, Joseph," she said, her voice filled with quiet strength. "I know we will."

Joseph looked at her, his eyes filled with tears. He nodded, his throat tight. "Yes," he said, his voice barely more than a whisper. "We will find a place."

They continued down the narrow streets, the sun dipping lower in the sky, the shadows lengthening around them. The crowded alleys seemed to close in, the noise of the city amplifying Joseph's sense of urgency. He could feel the pressure mounting, the time slipping away as Mary grew weaker with each step. The city seemed to close in on them, the noise, the crowds, the sense of urgency pressing down on Joseph's chest like a weight. He glanced at Mary, her steps growing slower, her breaths more labored, and he knew they were running out of time.

Finally, they came upon a small, rundown inn at the edge of the city, its walls weathered and cracked, a faint glow spilling from the open doorway. It seemed like a last chance—a glimmer of hope amidst the mounting despair. The door was open, the warm glow of a fire visible from within. Joseph approached, his heart pounding, his hand resting on the doorframe as he peered inside. An older woman stood by the hearth, her face lined with years, her eyes sharp as she looked up at them.

"Please," Joseph said, his voice trembling. "My wife is with child. We need a place to stay, even if it's just for the night."

The woman looked at Mary, her gaze softening. She stepped

closer, her eyes filled with concern as she took in the young woman's pale face and labored breathing. Her own eyes glistened with empathy, as if recognizing the desperate situation before her. "There is no room here," she said, her voice gentle. "But... there is a stable out back. It isn't much, but it will provide shelter."

Joseph's heart lifted, a spark of hope igniting within him. It wasn't much, but it was something—an answer to his silent prayers. Relief washed over him, and he turned to Mary, his eyes brimming with gratitude. He turned to Mary, his eyes filled with relief. She nodded, her lips curving into a small, grateful smile. "Thank you," Joseph said, his voice thick with emotion. "Thank you so much."

The woman nodded, her eyes warm. "Go, now. Rest. May the Almighty watch over you both. I will inform a midwife."

Joseph led Mary around the back of the inn, his arm wrapped around her shoulders, guiding her towards the stable. The scent of hay and animals filled the air, mingling with the earthy warmth of the stable. The soft glow of a lantern illuminated the small space, casting gentle shadows across the rough-hewn wooden walls. The animals shifted lazily in their pens, their quiet presence offering a strange sense of comfort. It was humble—the ground covered in straw, the animals' gentle breaths misting in the cool air—but it was shelter. It was a place where they could rest, where Mary could bring their child into the world. For that, Joseph was deeply grateful.

He helped Mary down, guiding her to a bed of hay, his hands gentle as he arranged the blankets around her. She looked up at him, her eyes filled with love, her lips curving into a soft smile, her fingers brushing against his. In this humble place, surrounded by the warmth of the animals and the quiet of the night, she felt a sense of peace—a feeling that, despite everything, they were where they needed to be. "We made it," she whispered, her voice barely audible. "We're here."

Joseph knelt beside her, his hand resting on her cheek, his

heart swelling with emotion. The exhaustion, the fear, the desperation of the day seemed to melt away, leaving only the anticipation of what was to come—the miracle they had both waited for. "Yes," he said, his voice thick with tears. "We're here. And soon, our child will be with us. He will be born here, in this humble stable, surrounded by love, and he will bring light to the world."

CHAPTER 13: A RESTLESS NIGHT

Joseph's eyes snapped open, his chest rising and falling with rapid breaths. The darkness of the stable pressed in around him, the scent of hay and the soft rustle of the animals filling the air. He sat up, his heart pounding, the remnants of a dream still clinging to his mind—shadowy figures with indistinct forms, their faces obscured, moving with deliberate intent. Joseph saw flashes of reaching hands, heard whispers that seemed to echo in his mind, and felt a cold dread that made his chest tighten. The figures loomed closer, their presence oppressive, and the overwhelming need to protect Mary and the child surged through him.

He glanced over at Mary, who lay on a bed of hay, her face peaceful in sleep, one hand resting protectively over her swollen belly. A wave of love and fear washed over him, the intensity of it almost overwhelming. The dream had felt so real, the sense of impending danger so palpable that it had jolted him awake. He couldn't shake the feeling that something was coming, something that threatened the safety of his family.

Joseph took a deep breath, running a hand through his hair, his eyes drifting to the small opening in the stable wall where the night sky was visible. The flickering lantern cast moving shadows across the wooden walls, and the rustle of the animals, the scent of hay mingling with the pungent odor of dung, filled the air. The wind howled softly outside, a distant owl's hoot adding to the unease in the stillness of the stable. The stars twinkled above, their light a reminder of the promise they were holding onto, the hope that had carried them this far. He knew that their journey was far from over, that the road ahead would be filled with challenges and uncertainties. But he also knew that he had to trust in the path they were on, that they were being guided by something far greater than themselves.

Mary stirred beside him, her eyes fluttering open, her gaze meeting his. She offered him a gentle smile, her voice soft and filled with warmth. "Joseph, are you alright?"

Joseph nodded, though the worry still lingered in his eyes. He took a deep breath, his gaze drifting towards the small opening in the stable. The sight of the stars above offered a flicker of reassurance, but his heart was still heavy with the weight of his fears. He wished he could shake the feeling of vulnerability, the sense that he had to be prepared for whatever lay ahead. He reached out, his hand resting gently on hers. "I had a dream," he said, his voice barely more than a whisper. "It felt so real… like a warning. I can't shake the feeling that we need to be careful, that danger is closer than we realize."

Mary's eyes softened, her hand tightening around his. She could see how deeply the dream had unsettled him, the burden he carried for their safety. Joseph's vulnerability was palpable, and she admired his strength even in these moments of fear. She knew that his love for her and the child was unwavering, even when faced with the unknown. She could see the fear in his eyes, the weight of the responsibility he felt. She knew how much he worried for her, for the child, and it made her heart ache with love for him. "I believe that we are being watched over," she said, her voice steady, filled with quiet conviction. "I know that there are dangers, but I also know that we are not alone. The child I carry is meant for something beyond our understanding, something greater than the fear we feel. And I have faith that we will be protected, even in the darkest of times.

Joseph looked at her, his heart swelling with emotion. Her faith was unwavering, a light cutting through the darkness of his fears. Her belief in the purpose of their journey was so strong, it seemed to reach out and calm the turmoil within him, reminding him of the promise they were holding onto—a promise that light would overcome darkness. He took a deep breath, his eyes searching hers, and he nodded. "You're right," he said, his voice filled with a mixture of awe and love. "I need to trust, just as you do. I need to believe that we are not alone."

Mary smiled, her eyes shining with warmth. She shifted, sitting up slightly, her hand resting on her belly. The rustling of hay beneath her and the warm presence of the animals around them created a sense of fragile comfort. The stable was humble, yet it felt like a sanctuary, a place where something extraordinary was about to unfold. "Do you want to feel him?" she asked, her voice filled with wonder.

Joseph's eyes widened, his breath catching in his throat. In this small, quiet moment amidst the uncertainty, he felt a mixture of awe and anticipation—despite the fears, there was a love so deep that it left him breathless. He nodded, his heart pounding with a mixture of excitement and fear. Mary took his hand, guiding it to her belly, and they both waited in silence. A moment later, Joseph felt it—a soft, gentle movement beneath his hand, a flutter of life that made his heart swell with awe.

"He's strong," Mary whispered, her eyes filled with tears. "And he knows that we love him, that we are doing everything we can to bring him safely into this world."

Joseph's eyes filled with tears, his heart aching with love. He looked at Mary, his voice thick with emotion. "I love you," he said, his voice barely more than a whisper. "And I love him, more than I ever thought possible. No matter what dangers we face, I will protect you both.""

Mary smiled, her eyes shining with love. "We are a family,

Joseph," she said. "And no matter what happens, we will face it together. The journey ahead may be uncertain, but we have each other, and we have faith. That is enough.""

CHAPTER 14: LEAH'S COMPASSION

"Hold on, little one," Leah whispered, her voice soothing as she dipped a cloth into a bowl of cool water. The scent of chamomile and yarrow wafted up from the bowl, the herbs chosen for their fever-reducing properties. The child lying before her let out a weak whimper, his skin flushed and hot to the touch. Leah's heart clenched as she placed the damp cloth on his forehead, hoping to bring him some relief. The small room was dimly lit, the air thick with the scent of thyme, rosemary, and sweat. Leah could hear the muffled voices of the child's parents, their anxious whispers drifting in from the next room, mixing with the crackle of a small fire in the hearth.

Leah wiped a strand of hair from her face, her brow furrowed in concentration. She mixed a poultice of crushed feverfew and willow bark, her hands moving deftly as she worked. The earthy aroma filled the room, and Leah hummed softly, her voice steady as she focused on her task. She had been tending to the sick for as long as she could remember, learning the ways of healing from her mother and the other midwives in their village. But no matter how many times she did this, it never got easier—the fear, the uncertainty, the knowledge that sometimes, despite her best efforts, she could do nothing but watch as the illness took its toll.

The child's mother entered the room, her eyes wide with worry, her hands wringing the edge of her shawl. "How is he?" she asked, her voice trembling. Leah looked up, her eyes softening as she met the woman's gaze. She could see the exhaustion etched on the mother's face, the fear that clung to her like a shadow.

"He's strong," Leah said, her voice calm and reassuring. "The fever will pass. We just need to keep him cool and let the herbs do their work."

The mother nodded, her eyes glistening with tears. She knelt beside her child, her hand resting gently on his chest, her lips moving in a silent prayer. Leah watched her, her heart aching with empathy. She knew what it was to feel helpless, to watch someone you loved suffer and know there was little you could do to ease their pain. It was a feeling that had driven her to become a healer, to do whatever she could to help others, even when the odds were against them.

The door to the small house creaked open, and Leah turned, her eyes widening as she saw Miriam, one of the elder midwives, standing in the doorway. Miriam's face was lined with age, her eyes sharp and filled with wisdom. She nodded to Leah, her lips curving into a small smile. "You're doing well, child," she said, her voice warm. "But I have news—news that may concern us all."

Leah rose to her feet, her heart pounding with a mixture of curiosity and apprehension. She glanced at the child's mother, who looked up, her eyes filled with questions. "What is it, Miriam?" Leah asked, her voice barely more than a whisper.

Miriam stepped further into the room, her gaze drifting to the child, her eyes lingering on the feverish flush before she looked back at Leah. The air seemed to shift, a sense of urgency filling the small space. "There is a woman—a young woman who may need help. She is staying in our stable, as there was no room at the inn, and she is with child. I thought you might want to know."

Leah's heart skipped a beat, her mind racing. A mixture of anticipation and fear swirled within her—she had seen the risks of childbirth many times, the fine line between life and death. Yet, there was also something else, a sense that this moment was significant, that perhaps this young woman was part of something greater. A young woman, with child, traveling through the harsh terrain—it was dangerous, especially so late in her pregnancy. Leah knew the risks—how easily things could go wrong, how fragile life was during childbirth, especially without proper shelter or support. She looked at Miriam, her eyes filled with determination, a spark of resolve igniting within her. "Where are they now?" she asked, her voice steady.

Miriam smiled, a glint of pride in her eyes. "They are here, Leah. They are in our stable. My husband and I offered them what little shelter we could, but the young woman needs help."

Leah's breath caught in her throat, her heart aching at the thought of a young mother, vulnerable and weary, about to give birth without proper shelter or care. She imagined the cold, the discomfort, the fear that must be gripping her. She looked at the child lying before her, his feverish face softening as the cool cloth brought him relief. She knew she couldn't leave the boy now—he still needed her. But the thought of the young woman, alone and vulnerable, tugged at her heart.

"I will go," Leah said, her voice filled with resolve. "As soon as the boy is well enough, I will go to the stable. If they need help, I will be there."

Miriam nodded, her eyes filled with approval and something else—an unspoken hope, a belief that perhaps Leah's compassion could make all the difference. "You have a kind heart, Leah," she said. "But remember, you cannot do everything on your own. There are others who can help. Trust in that, and trust in the path that has been laid before you."

Leah took a deep breath, her eyes drifting to the window,

to the night sky beyond. The stars twinkled above, their light piercing the darkness—a reminder that even in the most difficult moments, hope remained. She felt a quiet resolve settle within her. She could see the faint glow of the stars, their light a reminder of the hope that lay beyond the darkness. She knew that the situation would not be easy, that there would be challenges and dangers in helping a young mother give birth in a stable. But she also knew that she could not turn away—not when someone needed her, not when there was a chance she could make a difference.

The child's mother looked up at Leah, her eyes filled with gratitude. "Thank you," she whispered, her voice thick with emotion. "For everything."

Leah smiled, her heart swelling with warmth. She knew that her work, however small it seemed, was part of something greater—bringing light into the darkness, one life at a time. She knelt beside the child once more, her hand resting gently on his forehead. "Rest now," she said, her voice soft, filled with quiet assurance. "You are strong, and you will get through this. There is light ahead, even when it feels far away.""

CHAPTER 15: SALOME'S RELUCTANCE

"You're really going through with this?" Salome's voice was heavy with skepticism as she watched Leah pack a small bag. Leah paused, glancing over her shoulder at the older woman, her eyes filled with determination.

"Yes," Leah said simply, her hands moving steadily as she folded a cloth. "I have to go, Salome. There's a woman out there who needs help, and I can't ignore that."

Salome sighed, shaking her head. She leaned against the doorframe, her arms crossed over her chest. Her eyes were shadowed, filled with a deep and painful weight that had taken root long ago. Memories of loss, of broken dreams, clung to her, shaping her hardened exterior. "You don't even know her, Leah. For all you know, this could be a fool's errand. You might get there and find there's nothing you can do"

Leah looked up, her gaze meeting Salome's. There was compassion in her eyes, but also a quiet strength. "Maybe," she admitted. "But I have to try.

Salome frowned, her lips pressing into a thin line. She wanted to argue, to remind Leah that the world could be cruel, that people who tried to help often paid a heavy price. Her own experience had taught her that hope was dangerous, that it could shatter a person when reality struck. But deep down, Salome knew that Leah's heart was in the right place, and that was what made it so difficult. She envied Leah's hope, her unwavering belief that she could make a difference. It was a belief Salome had once held herself, long ago, before the weight of her own past had crushed it out of her.

Salome turned away, her eyes misting as memories flooded her mind—memories of a time when she had believed in miracles, believed that her hands could make a difference. She remembered the children she had delivered, the mothers she had comforted. And then there was the day she had lost them both—the screams, the blood, the helplessness that had shattered her spirit. It was the day she had learned that hope could be a cruel deceiver. She had been young, like Leah, filled with hope and determination. She had traveled to distant villages, offering her skills as a midwife, her heart filled with compassion for those in need. And then, there had been that one day, that one birth that had gone wrong. The screams, the blood, the helplessness as she watched the life slip away before her eyes. It had shattered something inside her, something she had never been able to mend.

"Salome?" Leah's voice was gentle, pulling her back from the dark recesses of her mind. Leah had stepped closer, her eyes filled with concern. "You don't have to come with me. I understand if you want to stay."

Salome closed her eyes, taking a deep breath. She felt the familiar ache in her chest, the weight of her past pressing down on her—the heartbreak that had made her cynical, the fear of failing again. She feared the fragility of life, the feeling of being powerless in the face of suffering. Part of her wanted to stay behind, to avoid the pain of watching another birth, to avoid the risk of reliving her worst fears. She could still hear the cries, still see the faces of those she had failed. But another part of her—a small, fragile part—wanted to believe that maybe this time would be different. But another part of her—a small, fragile part—wanted to believe that maybe, just maybe, she could find healing in helping Leah. Maybe if she faced her fears, she could find a way to move past the pain that had haunted her for so long.

Salome opened her eyes, her gaze meeting Leah's. There was a vulnerability there, a hint of the fear that she tried so hard to keep hidden. "I'll come with you," she said, her voice barely more than a whisper. "But don't expect me to be as hopeful as you are. I've seen what happens when hope is all you have—it's a dangerous thing, Leah. It can break you when it doesn't come true.""

Leah nodded, her eyes softening. She reached out, her hand resting gently on Salome's arm. "I don't expect you to be anything but yourself, Salome," she said. "And I appreciate you coming with me, more than you know."

Salome looked away, her throat tightening with emotion. She wanted to tell Leah that she was terrified, that she wasn't sure she could face her own ghosts again. But the words caught in her throat, and instead, she simply nodded, her eyes fixed on the dusty ground beneath her feet. But the words wouldn't come, and instead, she simply nodded, her eyes fixed on the floor.

✽ ✽ ✽

The walk to the stable was slow and heavy, the weight of the past pressing down on Salome with each step. The cold winter air seemed to cling to them, and the dusty path ahead mirrored the barrenness Salome often felt inside.

Leah glanced over at Salome, her brow furrowed in concern. "Are you alright?" she asked, her voice gentle, filled with the warmth that made her different from anyone Salome had known in years.

"Maybe you're right," Salome said, her voice barely audible. "Maybe there is still hope—even if it feels far away.""

CHAPTER 16: THE BIRTH OF JESUS (PART I)

"Breathe, Mary. Just breathe," Leah's voice was calm but edged with urgency as she knelt beside Mary, her hand resting on her shoulder. The air in the stable was thick, filled with the scent of hay, the soft rustling of the animals, and an almost electric sense of expectation, as if the very air was alive with anticipation. Miriam, the innkeeper's wife, stood near the doorway, her face a mixture of concern and awe. She had offered what little shelter she could to the young couple, and now she watched, her heart pounding, knowing that something truly special was unfolding here. The dim light of a single lantern cast flickering shadows across the walls, giving the small space a sense of intimacy that felt almost sacred.

Mary's face was flushed, her brow slick with sweat, her breaths coming in short, pained gasps. She clutched Leah's hand, her fingers trembling as another contraction rippled through her body, her eyes squeezed shut against the pain. Leah watched her, her heart aching with a mixture of fear and admiration. She had seen many births, had helped countless mothers bring their children into the world, but there was something different about this moment—something that made her chest tighten with a sense of awe.

Salome stood nearby, her arms crossed over her chest, her eyes fixed on Mary. Beside her, Miriam's gaze flickered between Leah and Mary, her hands clasped tightly in front of her as if in silent prayer. The stable felt different tonight, almost as if it were a sacred space, and both women couldn't shake the feeling that something extraordinary was happening. She had been hesitant to come, her heart still heavy with doubt, her mind filled with memories of her own past, of the pain that had made her question everything she had once believed. But as she watched Mary, her body wracked with pain, her face etched with determination, Salome felt something shift inside her—a softening, a crack in the armor she had built around her heart. Watching Mary's unwavering strength, she felt an unfamiliar sensation: a sense of awe, and perhaps even a whisper of faith returning, unbidden and tentative.

"She's doing well," Leah said, her voice steady, her eyes never leaving Mary's face. "You're strong, Mary. You're almost there."

Mary nodded, her breath hitching as she let out a low moan, her body tensing with the effort. Amid the pain, her thoughts turned inward—she prayed silently, trusting in God's plan, feeling both fear and an overwhelming love for the life she was about to bring into the world. She could feel the life within her, the child moving, the sense that he was ready to come into the world. The promise of the angel's words echoed in her mind, a reminder that this was no ordinary birth—this was part of something much greater. She took a deep breath, her heart filled with love, her mind focused on the promise that lay ahead.

Salome took a step closer, her eyes softening as she watched Leah work. There was something almost ethereal about Leah's calmness, the way her hands moved with precision, her voice filled with compassion. It reminded Salome of the woman she used to be—one who believed she could make a difference. There was a tenderness in Leah's actions, a quiet strength that seemed to fill the room, and for the first time in a long time, Salome felt a flicker of hope—a sense that maybe, just maybe, there was still light to be found in the world.

"Leah," Salome said, her voice barely a whisper, her eyes meeting Leah's. "What can I do?"

Leah looked up, her eyes filled with gratitude, and for a moment, Salome saw something in Leah's gaze that made her heart clench—an unspoken belief that they were witnessing a miracle. Miriam stepped forward, her voice trembling slightly. "Is there anything else I can do?" she asked, her eyes wide with both fear and hope. Leah nodded toward the basin of water, her voice gentle. "Bring the cloth. She'll need it soon." Miriam moved quickly, her hands shaking slightly as she picked up the cloth and handed it to Salome."

Salome moved quickly, her hands steady as she took the cloth from Miriam, her heart pounding in her chest. Despite her skepticism, there was an undeniable pull—a sense that she was meant to be here, in this moment, helping this young mother. Miriam knelt beside them, her eyes filled with wonder, her lips moving in a silent prayer. Salome knelt beside Mary, her eyes meeting the young woman's, her heart swelling with a mixture of fear and admiration. She knelt beside Mary, her eyes meeting the young woman's, her heart swelling with a mixture of fear and admiration. Mary looked at her, her eyes filled with pain but also with a deep, unwavering faith—a faith that seemed to fill the room, to wrap around them like a warm embrace.

"Thank you," Mary whispered, her voice thick with emotion, her eyes shining with tears. "Thank you for being here."

Salome swallowed hard, her throat tightening as she nodded, her eyes misting. "You are strong, Mary," she said, her voice trembling. "You are so strong."

The minutes seemed to stretch on forever, each contraction more intense than the last. The air in the stable was thick with the weight of the moment, as if all of creation was holding its breath, waiting for this child—this promise—to enter the world. Leah, Salome, and Miriam worked together, their movements fluid, their hands steady as they helped Mary through the pain, their voices calm and reassuring. Miriam's eyes were filled with tears, her heart aching with both fear and hope as she witnessed the strength of the young mother before her. Leah and Salome worked together, their movements fluid, their hands steady as they helped Mary through the pain, their voices calm and reassuring. And as the first light of dawn began to break over the horizon, a soft cry filled the stable—a cry so pure, so filled with life, that it seemed to reverberate through the very walls, touching something deep within each of them. Leah smiled through her tears, while Salome's heart swelled with emotions she could barely understand—a mix of awe, hope, and something that felt like the beginning of faith. Miriam clasped her hands to her chest, tears streaming down her cheeks as she whispered, "A miracle, truly a miracle." The atmosphere in the stable seemed to shimmer with an unspoken promise, a light that filled even the darkest corners of their hearts.

CHAPTER 17: THE BIRTH OF JESUS (PART II)

"**H**e's almost here," Leah whispered, her voice trembling with awe. The lantern light flickered, casting soft shadows along the stable's wooden beams, the interplay of light and shadow dancing across the walls as if celebrating the arrival of new life. Miriam, the innkeeper's wife, stood near the entrance, her eyes wide with awe as she watched. Mary's cries echoed off the walls, mingling with the occasional snort of the animals, the crackle of the lantern's flame, and the rustle of hay as the animals shifted restlessly. The air was heavy with anticipation, as if all creation was waiting with bated breath. Joseph stood by Mary's side, his face etched with both worry and hope. He clenched his hands, his knuckles white as he watched Leah and Miriam assist Mary. His heart raced, a mixture of fear for Mary and an overwhelming sense of awe at the life that was about to arrive. He whispered words of encouragement to Mary, his voice barely audible, filled with love and reverence.

When the baby's cries finally broke the silence, Joseph felt his heart swell to the point of bursting. Tears filled his eyes as he looked at his son, his vision blurring as emotions overwhelmed him. He knelt beside Mary, his hand gently resting on her shoulder, his gaze fixed on the tiny infant she held in her arms. Mary's tears flowed freely as she reached out, her hands trembling as she took the baby from Leah. She held him close, her heart bursting with love as she looked into his tiny face, his eyes blinking open for the first time. She could see the promise of hope in those eyes, a light that seemed to radiate from his very being, a warmth that contrasted with the coolness of the night air, filling her heart with a love beyond words.

The stable was quiet, the air filled with a profound stillness, as if time itself had paused to bear witness to the sacred moment. Even the animals seemed aware of the significance, their movements stilled, their eyes turned toward the source of the soft wail, as if in reverence. Joseph, still kneeling beside Mary, could hardly believe what he was seeing. He had heard Mary's words about the angel's message, but witnessing this moment, feeling the sacredness of the air around them, made it all real in a way he could never have imagined. He reached out, gently touching his son's tiny hand, and a soft smile spread across his face, tears rolling down his cheeks. Miriam stood beside Leah, her eyes glistening, her lips moving in a silent prayer of gratitude. Salome watched, her heart swelling with emotions she could barely comprehend—wonder, reverence, and an unfamiliar but welcome warmth, as if a long-forgotten hope had been reignited within her. She could feel the sacredness of the moment, the sense that they were witnessing something far greater than themselves. Salome watched, her heart swelling with emotions she could barely comprehend—wonder, reverence, and an unfamiliar but welcome warmth, as if a long-forgotten hope had been reignited within her. She could feel the sacredness of the moment, the sense that they were witnessing something far greater than themselves.

As Mary cradled her son, a light began to filter through the cracks in the stable walls—a soft, ethereal glow that seemed to come from the heavens themselves. Miriam gasped softly, her eyes widening as she saw the light grow stronger, illuminating the stable with a golden radiance. Joseph looked up, his eyes filled with wonder as the stable seemed to glow with an ethereal light. It was as if the heavens themselves were reaching down to touch this humble place, to bear witness to the miracle unfolding within. He glanced at Mary, who was gazing at their son, and his heart filled with a deep, unshakeable love for his family. He felt the weight of the moment, the knowledge that their lives had forever changed, and that this tiny child would bring hope to so many. She stepped back, her hand resting over her heart, her breath catching in her throat. She stepped back, her hand resting over her heart, her breath catching in her throat.

Outside, the star shone brightly in the sky, its light unlike anything the world had ever seen. Its radiance bathed the stable, casting a warm glow that felt almost tangible, as though the heavens themselves were offering their blessing. It bathed the stable in its glow, a beacon that seemed to call out to all who were weary, to all who needed hope. Even the animals, sensing the importance of the moment, grew still. The donkey knelt, the sheep lowered their heads, and the cow shifted gently, as if bowing in reverence to the tiny child who lay in Mary's arms, their forms bathed in the golden glow that filled the stable.

Salome looked around, her eyes misting as she saw the animals bow, their forms bathed in the heavenly light. Beside her, Miriam knelt, tears streaming down her cheeks as she whispered, "A miracle, truly a miracle." Joseph turned his gaze to Leah, Salome and Miriam, his heart swelling with gratitude for the women who had helped his wife through the labor. He nodded to them, his voice thick with emotion. "Thank you" he said quietly. Salome took a deep breath, her heart swelling with a sense of peace she hadn't felt in so long—a peace that whispered of miracles and rekindled faith. She took a deep breath, her heart swelling with a sense of peace she hadn't felt in so long. She had entered this night filled with doubt, her faith shaken by years of sorrow, but now, as she knelt in the presence of this child, she felt her heart begin to heal. The cracks that had once seemed irreparable were mending, a warmth spreading through her that whispered of hope—hope that perhaps, just perhaps, there was still light in this world.

"Mary," Leah whispered, her voice filled with awe, her eyes glistening with tears. "Look at him. He is truly a gift from the Almighty."

Mary looked down at her son, her heart swelling with love as she traced her fingers along his tiny cheek, her eyes filled with wonder. "He is more than a gift," she whispered, her voice trembling. "He is hope. He is the light that will guide us all."

Salome watched Mary, her heart aching with love for the young mother, for the courage she had shown, for the hope she had brought into the world. Miriam moved closer, her own heart filled with admiration for the young woman she had offered shelter to. Salome reached out, her hand resting gently on Mary's shoulder, her voice barely more than a whisper. "Thank you, Mary. Thank you for letting us be a part of this."

Mary looked up, her eyes filled with gratitude, her lips curving into a soft smile. She glanced at Joseph, who smiled back at her, his eyes still glistening with tears. "Thank you both," she said, her voice thick with emotion. "I couldn't have done this without you." Joseph nodded, his heart full, and he placed a gentle kiss on Mary's forehead. "We did this together," he whispered, his voice cracking with emotion. "And now, we have him.""

Leah knelt beside them, her eyes filled with tears, her heart swelling with a sense of purpose and reverence. Beside her, Miriam wiped her eyes, her lips trembling as she whispered a prayer of thanks. They knew that this was not merely the birth of a child—it was the birth of hope itself, a light to guide all who had wandered in darkness. Leah looked at the tiny baby, his eyes closed, his breathing soft and steady, and she knew that this was just the beginning—that this child, this tiny miracle, would grow to be something far greater than any of them could imagine.

"Welcome to the world, my son," Mary whispered, her voice filled with love. "May you bring light to all who seek it, and hope to those who have lost their way.""

CHAPTER 18: THE SHEPHERDS' NIGHT

Eli's breath was visible in the cold night air as he crouched beside the fire, his hands extended toward the crackling flames. His fingers trembled slightly, more from the unease that lingered in the stillness of the night than from the cold itself. The sheep rested around him, their woolly forms glowing in the flickering light. The other shepherds murmured quietly nearby, their voices a low hum that blended with the gentle rustling of the wind across the fields. The night had been quiet—too quiet, perhaps. It was the kind of quiet that made Eli's skin prickle with an uneasy awareness, as if the air itself was holding its breath, waiting for something. He exchanged glances with Nathan, his fellow shepherd, who looked just as unsettled, their eyes reflecting the dim glow of the fire.

Suddenly, a strange light cut through the darkness, illuminating the fields with an intensity that stole Eli's breath. He stumbled backward, his heart racing, the brilliant glow so intense that he had to shield his eyes with his arm. He looked up, his heart pounding, his eyes wide as he saw a light unlike any he had ever seen—a brilliant glow that seemed to pulse and shift, bathing everything in a golden radiance that filled his chest with both awe and fear. Beside him, Nathan's mouth fell open, his eyes darting between the sky and Eli, seeking some kind of explanation for the impossible sight.

"Eli!" Nathan's voice broke through the haze, and Eli turned to see his friend standing, his face lit by the same ethereal glow, his eyes filled with both wonder and terror. "Do you see this?"

Eli nodded, his eyes fixed on the sky, his heart pounding in his chest. He remembered the sign—the star that had appeared in the sky, brighter than any he had ever seen. And now, he saw them—figures within the light, their forms glowing, their wings spreading out like beams of light. The world seemed to hold its breath as a voice filled the air, a voice that was both gentle and commanding, resonating deep within Eli's heart. He felt his knees weaken, a primal instinct urging him to fall to the ground in the face of such overwhelming presence.

"Do not be afraid," the voice said, and Eli felt his fear begin to ease, replaced by a warmth that spread through his chest, melting away the icy dread that had gripped him only moments before. "For behold, I bring you good news of great joy that will be for all the people. Today in the town of David, a Savior has been born to you; He is the Messiah, the Lord."

Eli's mouth fell open, his eyes widening as the words sank in. A Savior? The Messiah? Eli's heart swelled with something he had not felt in so long—hope. He glanced at Nathan, whose eyes were wide with awe, tears brimming as the words took hold of their meaning. The promise they had heard in stories, whispered by elders, was now real. It was as if the weight of years of hardship, of fear and uncertainty, was lifted from his shoulders, replaced by a lightness that made tears fill his eyes.

Suddenly, the sky was filled with more light, with more voices —an entire host of heavenly beings, their figures ethereal, their voices raised in song. The melody was so beautiful that it made Eli's chest tighten, his breath catching in his throat. He felt tears spill down his cheeks, unable to contain the overwhelming sense of awe and reverence. The other shepherds stood beside him, trembling with awe, their eyes glistening with tears as they looked up at the sky. One of them, Reuben, whispered a prayer, his voice cracking, while another, Amos, clutched his staff as if to steady himself against the wonder before them.

"Glory to God in the highest heaven," the voices sang, their words filling the night with a sense of reverence and joy, "and on earth peace to those on whom his favor rests."

The song seemed to last for an eternity, and yet, when it ended, it felt too soon, the beauty of the moment leaving an aching emptiness in its absence. Eli's heart ached, longing to hold onto the light and the music, to capture the feeling of being part of something divine. The light began to fade, the sky returning to its deep, velvety darkness, the stars twinkling above as if nothing had happened. But everything had changed. Eli could feel it in his bones, in the way his heart seemed to beat with a new purpose.

Nathan turned to Eli, his eyes wide, his face flushed with excitement. "Did you hear that?" he asked, his voice trembling with both disbelief and joy. "The Messiah! The Savior is here! After all these years… He's really here!"

Eli nodded, a smile breaking across his face, his heart filled with a joy he had never known. "We have to go," he said, his voice steady, filled with a sense of purpose. "We have to see him. We have to see the child."

The other shepherds nodded, their faces filled with determination, a fire ignited in their hearts. Reuben wiped his eyes, his voice cracking as he said, "We cannot waste time. We must go now." They gathered what little they had—a few blankets, a small loaf of bread—and began to make their way across the fields, their footsteps quick, their hearts pounding with excitement. The sheep bleated softly as they were left behind, but Eli barely noticed, his mind focused on one thing—the child, the Savior, the hope they had been waiting for.

The journey to Bethlehem was filled with a sense of urgency, the cold night air biting at their faces, their breaths coming in short, visible puffs. Eli kept his eyes on the sky, the bright star shining above them like a beacon, guiding them to where they needed to be. The sheep bleated softly behind them, fading into the distance, while the sky above seemed to glow with the remnants of heavenly light, guiding their path. The fields gave way to the outskirts of the town, the dim lights of the houses flickering in the distance, casting long shadows over the cobblestones. Eli felt his heart swell with anticipation, his steps quickening as the realization dawned—soon, they would see the child, the hope that had been promised. They were close. They were so close.

CHAPTER 19: THE SHEPHERDS' JOURNEY

"Hurry, Eli! The star is still shining!" Nathan's voice cut through the cold night, his breath clouding in the crisp air. Eli adjusted the bundle of cloth he carried under his arm—a modest collection of herbs, dried fruits, and a small woven blanket, a humble offering for the child they had been told about. The fields around them stretched out in an endless sea of shadow, the frost-covered earth crunching beneath their hurried footsteps.

The other shepherds followed behind, their faces alight with excitement, their hearts filled with a mixture of awe and anticipation. The night had taken a miraculous turn, transforming from an ordinary watch over their flocks into something far beyond what they had ever imagined. The angelic proclamation still echoed in Eli's mind—words of hope, of a Savior born for all people. It had been a moment that shifted something deep within him, a promise that even in the midst of the darkness, there was light.

Eli glanced up at the sky, his eyes tracing the bright star that shone above them, its light unlike any he had ever seen before.

It seemed to guide them, to beckon them onward, and he felt a sense of purpose that propelled his tired legs forward. They had to reach the stable. They had to see the child.

As they entered the outskirts of Bethlehem, the narrow streets were quiet, the world around them still wrapped in the deep embrace of night. The houses were dark, their occupants long asleep, unaware of the miracle that had unfolded nearby. Eli's heart pounded in his chest as they approached the small, humble stable, its wooden frame bathed in the soft glow of the star above.

Nathan stepped forward, his hand resting on the door of the stable, his breath catching in his throat. He looked back at Eli, his eyes wide, his voice a whisper. "Do you think we're ready?"

Eli nodded, his gaze steady. "We must be," he said, his voice filled with quiet determination. "This is what we were called to do."

Nathan pushed the door open, the creaking of the wood echoing in the stillness. The soft glow of a lantern illuminated the small space, the scent of hay and animals filling the air. Eli's eyes widened as he took in the scene before him—Mary, her face radiant with love, cradling her newborn son, Joseph by her side, his eyes filled with awe. As he gazed at his newborn son, he felt a profound sense of peace and joy—a moment of divine fulfillment that surpassed anything he had ever imagined.

The child lay wrapped in swaddling clothes, his tiny face peaceful, his eyes closed in slumber. Joseph knelt beside Mary, his gaze never leaving his son's face, overwhelmed by the significance of the moment. Eli stepped forward, his hands trembling as he knelt before the child, his heart pounding in his chest. He placed his bundle beside the manger, his eyes fixed on the tiny face before him. The child was so small, so vulnerable, and yet Eli could feel the weight of the moment, the sense that they were in the presence of something far greater than themselves.

Nathan knelt beside him, his eyes filled with tears, his voice barely more than a whisper. 'We brought what we could,' he said, his voice trembling. 'It isn't much, but it's all we have.' Joseph's eyes softened, filled with gratitude for the shepherds' simple yet heartfelt offering. Mary smiled, her eyes shining with gratitude. 'It is more than enough,' she said, her voice filled with warmth. 'Your presence here is a gift in itself.' Joseph nodded sincerely. 'You honor us with your presence.'

The other shepherds gathered around, their faces filled with awe, their eyes glistening with tears as they looked at the child. The soft cries of the animals filled the air, the warmth of their bodies creating a cocoon of comfort in the cold of the night. Eli could feel the sacredness of the moment, the sense that they were witnessing a miracle—something that would change the world.

He looked at Mary, her face glowing with love as she held her son close, and he felt a sense of hope unlike anything he had ever known. Joseph's hand rested gently on Mary's shoulder, his eyes filled with emotion. The weight of the journey seemed to lift, replaced by a lightness and joy that filled every part of him.

Nathan leaned closer, his eyes fixed on the baby, his voice filled with wonder. "Is this truly the Messiah?" he asked, his voice trembling. "The one we've been waiting for?"

Mary nodded, her eyes filled with tears, her voice barely more than a whisper. "He is," she said, her gaze drifting down to her son. "He is the hope of all people."

Eli closed his eyes, his heart swelling with gratitude, his mind filled with the words the angel had spoken—good news of great joy for all people. He took a deep breath, his eyes opening to look at the child once more, his heart filled with a sense of purpose. This was what they had been waiting for. This was the light that would guide them, the hope that would carry them through the darkest of times.

The stable was filled with a profound stillness, the only sound the soft breathing of the baby, the gentle rustling of the animals, the quiet sobs of the shepherds as they knelt in reverence. Eli looked around at his friends, their faces etched with awe, their eyes filled with tears, and he knew that they all felt the same—that this was a moment they would carry with them for the rest of their lives. Joseph watched the shepherds, feeling a deep connection to them—a shared reverence for the child who had brought them all together in this humble stable.

Nathan reached out, his fingers brushing against the small woven blanket they had brought, his eyes glistening with tears. Joseph watched as Nathan gently placed the blanket beside the baby, grateful for their kindness. 'It's not much,' Nathan whispered, his voice breaking. 'But it's from our hearts.' Mary looked at him, her eyes filled with warmth, her voice gentle. 'It is perfect,' she said, her eyes shining with gratitude. 'He will be wrapped in love, and that is the greatest gift of all.' Joseph smiled, nodding at Nathan and the other shepherds. 'Your kindness will always be remembered,' he said warmly.

Eli felt tears slip down his cheeks, his heart filled with a sense of wonder, of joy that seemed to overflow. He looked up at the star shining above, its light streaming through the stable, bathing them all in its glow, and he knew that they were not alone—that they were part of something far greater than themselves.

The shepherds stayed for a while longer, their hearts too full to leave, their eyes fixed on the tiny child who lay in the manger, his presence filling the stable with warmth and light. They spoke softly to one another, sharing their hopes, their fears, their dreams for the future—a future that seemed a little brighter now, a little more hopeful.

Eli knelt beside Nathan, his voice filled with reverence, his eyes never leaving the child. "This changes everything," he whispered, his heart swelling with hope. "This child… He will bring light to the world. He will guide us."

Nathan nodded, his eyes glistening with tears, his voice trembling. "Yes," he said, his voice filled with conviction. "He is the hope we have been waiting for."

Eli took a deep breath, his heart filled with gratitude, his eyes fixed on the tiny child who had brought them all together. He knew that this was just the beginning—that the journey ahead would be filled with challenges, with moments of doubt and fear. But he also knew that they were not alone, that the light they had seen, the hope they had found, would guide them through whatever lay ahead.

As they rose to leave, Eli turned to Mary, his heart filled with love, his voice trembling. 'Thank you,' he said, his eyes filled with tears. 'Thank you for letting us be a part of this.' Mary smiled, her eyes shining with warmth, her voice soft. 'Thank you for coming,' she said. 'Your presence here means more than you know.' Joseph nodded. 'You will always be part of this story,' he added. 'We will never forget your kindness.'

Eli nodded, his heart filled with a sense of peace, his mind filled with hope. He looked at the child one last time, his heart swelling with love, and he knew that everything would be alright—that they were part of something far greater than themselves, something beautiful and extraordinary.

As the shepherds stepped out of the stable, the light of the star still shining brightly above, they felt the weight of the world lift from their shoulders, replaced by a sense of joy, of hope that filled every part of them. They had seen the Savior. They had knelt in His presence, and they knew that their lives would never be the same.

CHAPTER 20: THE MAGI'S ARRIVAL

Azar wiped the sweat from his brow. The journey had been arduous, filled with sleepless nights, harsh desert winds, and moments of uncertainty. They had crossed mountains and valleys, faced sandstorms, and endured the heat of the sun, but now, as they approached Bethlehem, the sight of the bright star above filled him with renewed purpose. It was a beacon, leading them to something far greater than they could have imagined. Beside him, his fellow Magi rode in silence, their eyes also fixed on the celestial light that had guided them across miles of desert.

The small town was settling for the evening, the air filled with the mingling sounds of daily life winding down. The scent of cooking fires drifted through the streets as they made their way past children playing in doorways, their laughter echoing off the stone walls, while women gathered water from a communal well. Azar could feel the weight of the people's curious stares—some filled with curiosity, others with suspicion—but he paid them no mind. His focus was on the stable, the place where the star's light seemed to rest, guiding them to their destination.

"Azar, do you see it?" Balthazar's voice broke through his thoughts, his tone a mixture of awe and exhaustion. He gestured towards a humble structure at the edge of the town, its roof thatched, its walls simple and unadorned. It was there that the star seemed to shine most brightly, its light spilling down like a waterfall of gold.

Azar nodded, his throat tight with emotion. "Yes, I see it," he replied, his voice barely a whisper. The doubts that had plagued him throughout their journey—questions of whether they were truly following a divine sign, whether this child could truly be the one they had read of in the ancient texts—began to fade away. He could feel something within him stir, a sense of wonder that he had not allowed himself to fully embrace until now.

They dismounted, the crunch of gravel beneath their feet the only sound as they approached the stable. The air was heavy with anticipation, the night still and quiet, as if the world itself held its breath for what was about to unfold. Melchior, his face lined with age and wisdom, carried a small chest of gold, while Balthazar held a vessel of myrrh. Azar carried his own gift—frankincense, its rich, aromatic scent filling the air around him. It was a gift for a king, a symbol of divinity, and as he held it close, he felt a strange sense of calm wash over him.

Balthazar reached the door first, his hand resting against the rough wood. He turned to Azar and Melchior, his eyes wide, a smile playing at the corners of his lips. 'Brothers, this is it,' he said, his voice trembling with emotion. 'This is the moment we have journeyed so far to witness.'

Azar swallowed, his heart pounding as the door creaked open. The stable was dimly lit, the soft glow of a lantern casting gentle shadows across the walls. The earthy scent of hay mixed with the warmth of the animals, and Azar felt the weight of the moment settle over him as he laid eyes on the humble scene before them. There, at the center of it all, was a young woman cradling a child, her face serene, her eyes filled with a love so deep it seemed to radiate from her very being.

Joseph, standing beside her, looked up as the Magi entered, his eyes widening in surprise. Mary turned, her gaze meeting Azar's, her expression one of warmth and welcome. She shifted slightly, revealing the child in her arms—tiny, fragile, his eyes closed, his breathing soft and steady.

Azar felt his breath catch in his throat, his heart swelling with a mixture of awe and reverence. He had imagined this moment so many times, had pictured what it would be like to look upon the face of the one they had traveled so far to find, but nothing could have prepared him for the reality of it. The child was so small, so vulnerable, and yet there was something about him—something that seemed to fill the entire room with light.

Melchior stepped forward first, his knees bending as he knelt before the child, his hands trembling as he placed the chest of gold at Mary's feet. "For the king of kings," he whispered, his voice thick with emotion. "A gift worthy of his majesty."

Balthazar followed, his vessel of myrrh held carefully in his hands. He knelt beside Melchior, his eyes glistening with tears. "For the healer of nations," he said, his voice breaking. "A symbol of the sacrifice he will one day make."

Azar took a deep breath, his hands shaking as he stepped forward, his eyes fixed on the child. He knelt, placing the frankincense beside the other gifts, his heart pounding in his chest. "For the divine," he whispered, his voice barely audible. "A gift for the one who will bring us closer to the Almighty."

Mary looked at each of them, her eyes filled with gratitude, her lips curving into a gentle smile. 'Thank you,' she said, her voice soft and filled with warmth. 'Your journey has brought you far, and your gifts are received with a grateful heart.'

Azar looked up at her, his doubts finally dissolving, his heart filled with a peace he had never known. He could see the love in Mary's eyes, the hope that she held for her son, and he knew, without a doubt, that they were in the presence of something sacred. This child was more than just a king—he was a beacon of hope, a light in the darkness, and Azar felt humbled to be a part of it.

As the Magi knelt in reverence, the stable seemed to glow with a warmth that came not from the lanterns, but from the presence of the child. The animals shifted quietly, their heads bowed, as if even they could sense the importance of the moment. The air was filled with a profound stillness, a sense of peace that wrapped around them like a comforting embrace.

Azar closed his eyes, his heart overwhelmed with reverence. He had questioned, he had doubted, but now, in this moment, all of that seemed to fade away, replaced by the certainty that they were exactly where they were meant to be. He opened his eyes, his gaze drifting to the child, and he felt a tear slip down his cheek, his soul brimming with tenderness.

Joseph stepped forward, his voice gentle, his eyes filled with awe. 'You have come from so far,' he said, his voice trembling. 'What brought you here?'

Melchior looked up, his eyes meeting Joseph's. "We followed the star," he said, his voice steady. "We have read the prophecies, we have seen the signs. We knew that something miraculous was happening, and we had to be a part of it."

Balthazar nodded, his eyes still fixed on the child. 'We came seeking a king,' he said, his voice filled with reverence. 'But we have found something far greater—a hope for all people, something that will transcend time and place.'

Azar smiled, his gaze drifting back to the child. 'We brought gifts fit for a king,' he said softly, 'but it is our hearts that have been filled—filled with the knowledge that hope has truly come into the world.'

Mary's eyes filled with tears, her voice trembling as she spoke. "He is here for all of us," she said, her voice filled with love. "For everyone who seeks him, for everyone who needs hope."

The Magi knelt in silence, their hearts filled with a sense of wonder, their eyes fixed on the tiny child who had brought them together. The light of the star shone brightly above, its glow filling the stable, casting a golden light over them all. Azar took a deep breath, his heart overflowing with awe, his mind filled with the knowledge that they were part of something far greater than themselves.

As they rose to leave, Azar turned to Mary, his heart filled with love, his voice trembling. "Thank you," he said, his eyes glistening with tears. "Thank you for allowing us to be a part of this."

Mary smiled, her eyes filled with warmth. "Thank you for coming," she said. "Your journey has brought you here, and your presence means more than you know."

Azar nodded, his heart filled with peace as he stepped out of the stable, the cold night air wrapping around him, the light of the star still shining above. He looked up at the sky, his heart filled with hope, and he knew that their journey was far from over—that this was just the beginning of something beautiful, something extraordinary.

And as the Magi made their way back through the quiet streets of Bethlehem, their hearts filled with love, their minds filled with hope, they knew that they were not alone—that the light they had seen, the hope they had found, would guide them through whatever lay ahead, and that the child they had knelt before this night would bring light to all people, a light that would never fade.

CHAPTER 21: A MOTHER'S REFLECTION

The stable was quiet now, the lantern's soft glow casting gentle light over the sleeping child. Mary cradled Jesus in her arms, her eyes tracing the lines of his tiny face—each delicate eyelash, each soft curve of his cheek. His breathing was gentle, rhythmic, and she could feel the warmth of him against her chest, the weight of his small body settling into her. The exhaustion of labor still lingered in her muscles, but there was a sense of serenity that filled her heart, a stillness that made every ache worth it.

Mary took a deep breath, her gaze shifting to the sky visible through the cracks in the stable's roof. The star still shone brightly, its light reaching down as if to touch them. She marveled at the miracle that had unfolded—the prophecy she had heard as a young girl now resting in her arms, a child whose presence seemed to carry the hopes and burdens of an entire world. She had believed in her heart that she was chosen, but now, as she held her son, the magnitude of it all washed over her in waves.

She leaned down, her lips brushing the Jesus head, an

overwhelming surge of fierce love she had never known.

Joseph stirred from where he sat, his eyes weary but filled with warmth as he looked at Mary and the baby. He rose quietly, crossing the stable to kneel beside them, his gaze fixed on Jesus. He reached out, his fingers brushing gently against the baby's tiny hand, a mixture of pride and trepidation welling within him.

"He's perfect," Joseph whispered, his voice filled with awe. "I can hardly believe he's here."

Mary looked up at Joseph, her eyes glistening with tears. 'He is,' she agreed, her voice barely audible. 'But sometimes I wonder if I am ready for this—if I am truly capable of being the mother he needs. The weight of his destiny, it scares me sometimes.'

Joseph's brow furrowed, and he reached out, his hand resting gently on Mary's shoulder. "You are more than capable, Mary," he said, his voice steady, his eyes filled with conviction. "You have a strength that I have never seen in anyone. And I will be here, by your side, to help you, to protect you both."

Mary smiled, a profound sense of gratitude filling her. She knew that Joseph carried his own burdens, his own fears. He had chosen to stay, to believe, even when the world around them questioned and doubted their journey. She knew the path ahead would not be easy, that there would be moments of fear and uncertainty, but she also knew that she was not alone—that they were not alone.

She looked back down at Jesus, her heart overflowing with tenderness as she watched his tiny chest rise and fall with each breath. 'Do you think he knows?' she asked, her voice soft, almost as if she were afraid to speak the words aloud. 'Do you think he knows who he is, what he is meant to do, the greatness that awaits him?'

Joseph was silent for a moment, his gaze fixed on the child. He took a deep breath, his heart heavy with the weight of the question. "I think he will learn," he said finally, his voice gentle.

"I think he will grow into his purpose, that he will come to understand in time. And until then, we will guide him, we will protect him, and we will love him with everything we have."

Mary nodded, her eyes filling with tears. She leaned her head against Joseph's shoulder, her heart filled with a mixture of hope and fear, of love and uncertainty. She knew that their journey was only just beginning—that there would be moments of great joy and moments of profound sorrow. But as she held her son close, she felt a sense of peace wash over her, a sense that they were part of something far greater than themselves.

The stable was quiet, the soft rustling of the animals the only sound. The light of the star shone down on them, bathing them in its gentle glow, and Mary closed her eyes, her heart filled with a deep sense of gratitude and purpose. She knew that there would be challenges ahead, that the path they were on would not be easy. But she also knew that they had been chosen for this—that they had been given a gift, a chance to be part of a story that would change the world.

Joseph looked down at Mary, his devotion deepening as he watched her as he watched her hold their son. He knew that his role was to protect them, to guide them, and to be the unwavering support they could lean on. It was a responsibility that filled him with both pride and fear, but as he looked at his family, he knew that he would do whatever it took to keep them safe.

"We are blessed," Joseph said, his voice filled with emotion. "We have been given a gift that the world has been waiting for. And I will do everything in my power to protect you both."

Mary looked up at him, her eyes shining with love. "And I will do everything in my power to love him, to nurture him, to help him grow into the man he is meant to be."

They sat in silence for a moment, their hearts filled with love, their minds filled with the weight of the journey ahead. The star above continued to shine, its light a reminder of the hope that had been born this night, a hope that would guide them through whatever lay ahead.

Mary leaned down, her lips brushing against Jesus' forehead, her heart overwhelmed with love. 'Sleep, my son,' she whispered, her voice filled with tenderness. 'For tomorrow, we embark on a journey that will change the world.'

Joseph nodded, his resolve steady and unwavering. He knew that their journey was only beginning, that there would be trials, and that moments of fear and uncertainty lay ahead. But he also knew that they were not alone—that they were part of something far greater than themselves, something beautiful and extraordinary.

And as the night wore on, the stable filled with the soft glow of the star above, Mary and Joseph held their son close, their hearts filled with love, their minds filled with hope. They knew that the road ahead would be long, that there would be challenges they could not yet imagine. But they also knew that they had each other, that they had been given a gift that would guide them, that would light their way.

For tonight, that was enough.

CHAPTER 22: THE LIGHT SPREADS

"Did you hear?" The voice was filled with wonder, hushed and eager as a young woman leaned closer to her friend, her eyes wide with excitement. They stood at the well, their clay jars resting beside them, as the cool morning air wrapped around the village of Bethlehem. "A child has been born—a child like no other. They say he is the one the prophets spoke of."

Her friend, a middle-aged woman with lines etched into her face from years of hardship, raised her eyebrows, her hands pausing mid-draw as she pulled the rope attached to the heavy bucket. "The one? Are you sure?" she asked, her voice skeptical, but her eyes held a glimmer of hope. It had been so long since she had dared to hope for anything better.

"Yes," the young woman said, her eyes shining. "The shepherds have been telling everyone. They saw angels—angels, can you imagine? They say that a Savior has been born, and they went to see him in a stable, just outside the village."

The older woman's hands stilled, her pulse racing in her chest. Angels? A Savior? The words seemed almost too miraculous to believe, and yet, something in the young woman's face, in the way her eyes shone with hope, made her wonder if perhaps, just perhaps, it could be true.

The two women continued their work, but the air between them seemed to have shifted, filled now with a sense of possibility that had not been there before. The older woman drew the water from the well, filling her jar, and as she did, she glanced up at the sky, her heart whispering a quiet prayer—a prayer for hope, for light, for something more than the life she had known.

Word of the birth spread quickly through the village, carried on the whispers of shepherds, of travelers who had glimpsed the bright star that still hung in the sky. People spoke in hushed voices, their eyes wide with wonder, their spirits brimming with anticipation. The story of the child, born in a stable, seemed to ignite something within them—a spark of hope that began to ripple outward, touching everyone it encountered.

At the marketplace, a merchant named Haran listened to the whispers of his customers, his hands pausing as he wrapped a bolt of cloth in brown paper. "A Savior?" he repeated, his brow furrowing as he looked up at the group of women gathered at his stall. "And you say the shepherds saw angels?"

The women nodded, their faces alight with excitement. "They say the child is the one we have all been waiting for," one of them said, her voice trembling with emotion. "He is the Messiah, born here in Bethlehem."

Haran swallowed, his heart heavy with the weight of the words. He had lived through so much—through Roman oppression, through the struggles of making a living, through the loss of his family. He had seen hope dashed time and again, and yet now, as he listened to the voices of those around him, he felt something stir within him—a tiny flicker of hope that refused to be extinguished.

He looked down at the coins in his hand, his heart pounding in his chest. Slowly, he pushed the coins back toward the woman who had come to buy cloth. "Take it," he said, his voice rough with emotion. "Take it as a gift. Let it be a symbol of the hope that has been born today."

The woman's eyes filled with tears, her hand trembling as she reached out to take the cloth. "Thank you, Haran," she whispered, her voice thick with emotion. "Thank you."

Haran nodded, his heart surging with a sense of purpose he had not felt in so long. He watched as the woman turned and walked away, the cloth held close to her chest, her eyes filled with tears of gratitude. He took a deep breath, his eyes drifting to the sky, the bright star still shining above, and he knew that this was only the beginning—that the hope that had been born this day would continue to spread, touching everyone it encountered.

At the edge of the village, a young boy named Daniel stood beside his father, their flock of sheep grazing nearby. He had heard the shepherds' story, had seen the excitement in their eyes, and he could feel his heart pounding with a sense of wonder. He turned to his father, his voice filled with excitement. "Can we go, Papa? Can we go see the child?"

His father hesitated, his brow furrowing. "It is not for us, Daniel," he said, his voice gentle but firm. "We are just shepherds. The child is meant for kings, for people far greater than us."

"But the shepherds went," Daniel said, his eyes wide, his voice trembling. "They saw angels, Papa. They said the child was born for all of us."

His father looked down at him, his heart heavy with the weight of his words. He had spent his life in the fields, tending to his flock, living a life of hardship and simplicity. The idea that a Savior could be born for him, for people like him, seemed almost too incredible to believe. And yet, as he looked into his son's eyes, he saw something that made his heart swell with love—a hope, a light that he had not seen in so long.

"Alright," he said finally, his voice soft, filled with emotion. "We will go. We will see the child."

Daniel's face lit up, his eyes shining with excitement. He grabbed his father's hand, his heart pounding with joy as they began to make their way toward the stable. The fields around them were quiet, the only sound the gentle bleating of their sheep, the rustling of the wind in the grass. And above them, the star shone brightly, its light guiding them, filling them with a sense of purpose.

As they approached the stable, Daniel's heart swelled with a mixture of awe and excitement. He could see the soft glow of lanterns spilling out from the cracks in the walls, the sound of quiet voices drifting on the wind. He stepped closer, his eyes widening as he caught sight of the young mother, her face serene, her eyes filled with love as she cradled her newborn son.

Daniel's father knelt beside him, his spirit filled with reverence as he looked at the child. He took a deep breath, his eyes filling with tears as he whispered a quiet prayer—a prayer of gratitude, of hope, of love. And as he looked up at the star above, he knew that this was just the beginning—that the hope that had been born this day would continue to spread, touching everyone it encountered, changing the world one heart at a time.

In the days that followed, the news of the birth continued to spread, carried on the whispers of those who had seen the star, who had heard the story of the child born in a stable. And as the story spread, so too did the hope, the light that seemed to touch everyone it encountered.

People began to perform small acts of kindness—gifts given freely, debts forgiven, food shared with those who had none. It was as if the light of the star had ignited something within them, a desire to be better, to love more deeply, to give more freely.

At the marketplace, Haran continued to give freely, his heart filled with a sense of purpose. He watched as people came and went, their faces filled with hope, their eyes shining with gratitude. He knew that the child born in the stable was more than just a baby—he was a symbol of hope, of a new beginning, and Haran felt honored to be a part of it.

The young women at the well spoke of the child, their voices filled with excitement, their spirits brimming with hope. They shared the story with everyone they met, their eyes shining with the light that had been born that night. And as they spoke, they could see the way people's faces softened, the way their eyes filled with tears, and they knew that they were part of something far greater than themselves.

Daniel and his father returned to their flock, their hearts filled with a sense of wonder. They spoke of the child, of the hope they had found, and they could feel the way it changed them—the way it made the world seem a little brighter, a little more hopeful.

And as the days turned into weeks, the light continued to spread, touching everyone it encountered, changing the world one heart at a time. The child born in a stable had brought hope to a world that had long been yearning for it, and the people of Bethlehem knew that they were part of something beautiful, something extraordinary.

The star still shone brightly above, a beacon of hope, a reminder of the light that had been born that night. And as the people of Bethlehem looked up at the sky, their hearts filled with love, their minds filled with hope, they knew that the world would never be the same—that the light that had been born that night would continue to guide them, to inspire them, to fill them with hope for all the days to come.

CHAPTER 23: HEROD'S RAGE

The torchlight flickered against the cold stone walls, casting long, wavering shadows that seemed to dance with a life of their own. Herod paced the length of his chamber, tension thick in the room. His eyes narrowed as the messenger knelt before him, head bowed low, while his footsteps echoed in the silence.

"What do you mean they did not return?" Herod's voice was low, dangerous, his eyes narrowing as he glared down at the messenger. His fingers clenched at his sides, his entire body taut as if ready to pounce.

The young man's head remained bowed, his voice trembling as he spoke. "My lord, the Magi have not returned as you requested. They... they were seen traveling back east, without coming to see you."

Herod's face darkened, a storm brewing behind his eyes. He could feel the heat of rage coursing through his veins, his heart pounding in his chest as the realization settled in. They had disobeyed him—those so-called wise men had dared to defy his orders. His jaw clenched, and he turned away from the messenger, his eyes staring blankly at the wall as his mind raced.

"Fools," he muttered under his breath, his voice barely audible.

"Do they think they can deceive me? Do they think I will let this go unpunished?"

He strode to the window, the cold night air biting at his skin as he looked out over the city. Bethlehem lay in the distance, quiet and unassuming, its lights twinkling like stars scattered across the landscape. He could feel the weight of the prophecy pressing down on him—the words of the ancient texts that spoke of a king, a Messiah who would rise and challenge his throne. It was a threat he could not ignore, a danger that had to be eliminated.

The messenger remained kneeling, his head bowed, his heart pounding in his chest. He had heard stories of Herod's wrath, tales of the lengths he would go to protect his power. He dared not move, dared not even breathe too loudly, for fear of drawing the king's ire.

Herod turned back to the messenger, his eyes cold, calculating. "Send for my advisors," he commanded, his voice like ice. "We must act swiftly. This child—this so-called king—must be found and eliminated before he becomes a threat."

The messenger nodded quickly, scrambling to his feet and bowing deeply before hurrying from the room, his footsteps echoing down the corridor. Herod watched him go, his mind already turning over the possibilities, the ways in which he could ensure that his throne remained secure.

He would not be made a fool of. He would not allow some prophecy to undo everything he had worked for, everything he had fought to build. His eyes narrowed, and he could feel the cold resolve settling in his chest, the determination that had carried him through countless battles, through years of political maneuvering and bloodshed.

No one would take what was his.

Moments later, the door to his chamber opened, and his advisors entered, their faces pale, their eyes filled with apprehension. They could see the tension in Herod's posture, the way his eyes burned with barely restrained fury. They exchanged nervous glances, their hearts heavy with the knowledge of what was to come.

Herod turned to face them, his gaze sweeping over the group, his voice calm, measured. "The Magi have defied me," he said, his eyes narrowing. "They have refused to return and inform me of the child's location. We cannot allow this threat to grow any further."

One of the advisors, an older man with a thin face and sunken eyes, stepped forward, his voice hesitant. "What would you have us do, my lord?"

Herod's gaze locked onto him, his lips curling into a cold smile. "We will root out this so-called king before he has a chance to rise," he said, his voice dripping with malice. "We will send our soldiers to Bethlehem, and we will leave no stone unturned. Every male child under the age of two will be put to the sword. We will ensure that this threat is eliminated before it has a chance to grow."

The room fell silent, the weight of Herod's words settling over them like a shroud. The advisors exchanged uneasy glances, their faces pale, their eyes filled with fear. They knew what this meant—they knew the bloodshed that would follow, the lives that would be lost. But they also knew that to question Herod was to invite his wrath, to risk their own lives.

The older advisor bowed his head, his voice barely more than a whisper. "It will be done, my lord."

Herod nodded, his eyes cold, devoid of any emotion. "See to it," he said, his voice like ice. "And make no mistake—anyone who stands in our way will be dealt with accordingly."

The advisors bowed deeply before turning and leaving the room, their hearts heavy with the knowledge of what they had been ordered to do. Herod watched them go, his eyes narrowing as he turned back to the window, his gaze fixed on the distant lights of Bethlehem.

He would not allow some child to threaten everything he had

built. He would do whatever it took to protect his throne, to ensure that his rule remained unchallenged.

The cold night wind swept through the room, rustling the heavy drapes as Herod stared out into the darkness, his heart filled with a dark resolve. He had faced threats before—rebellions, rivalries, enemies who had tried to take what was his. And each time, he had emerged victorious, his power unbroken, his rule secure.

This child would be no different.

As the night wore on, Herod's rage simmered beneath the surface, a dark, boiling force that threatened to consume him. He could feel it in the pit of his stomach, the anger, the fear—the knowledge that somewhere out there, a child had been born who was destined to take his place. It was a threat he could not ignore, a danger that had to be eliminated.

He would send his soldiers to ensure no child escaped, no family was spared. He would root out this threat and crush it before it had a chance to grow.

And when it was done, when the streets of Bethlehem ran red with the blood of the innocent, he would sleep soundly, knowing that his throne was secure, that his power remained unchallenged.

For Herod, there was no other way. There was no room for mercy, no place for compassion. There was only power—his power—and he would do whatever it took to protect it.

The flickering torchlight cast shadows across his face as he stared into the night, his resolve unyielding. The prophecy would not come to pass. The child would not live to see his throne. And Herod would remain king, his power unbroken, his rule secure.

Outside, the distant lights of Bethlehem twinkled in the darkness, unaware of the storm that was about to descend upon them. Unaware of the rage that had been ignited, the dark force that was gathering, ready to strike.

Herod turned away from the window, his eyes filled with a cold, unyielding resolve. He would not be defeated. He would not be overthrown.

And as the first light of dawn began to break over the horizon, Herod's heart was filled with a single, chilling thought—no one would take what was his. No one.

The massacre was only the beginning.

CHAPTER 24:
CASSIUS' CONSCIENCE

The scroll lay on the wooden table before Cassius, its edges curled slightly from the dampness that lingered in the air of the barracks. He stared at the words, his chest tightening as he read the command again and again, each time feeling the weight of it settle heavier upon his shoulders. The orders were clear—march to Bethlehem, execute the decree. No male child under the age of two was to be spared. It was the king's will.

Cassius ran a hand through his short-cropped hair, his jaw clenching as he looked away from the scroll, his eyes darting to the window, where the first light of dawn was beginning to filter through the narrow opening. The barracks were quiet, the men still resting before the day's march. He could hear the soft murmur of their sleep, the occasional rustle of someone shifting beneath a blanket. It was a rare, peaceful moment, but the words on the scroll had shattered any peace that Cassius could hope to feel.

He rose from his seat, the legs of the wooden chair scraping against the stone floor as he stood. He paced the length of the small room, his mind racing, his heart pounding. He had followed Herod's orders for years—he had fought in his wars, had defended his throne against all who sought to challenge him. He had done things he wished he could forget, things that haunted his dreams. But this—this was different. This was not a battle, not a rebellion. These were children.

He paused by the window, his hands resting on the rough stone ledge as he looked out over the city. The sun was just beginning to rise, casting a soft golden glow over the rooftops, the narrow streets still empty in the early morning light. In the distance, he could see the hills that led to Bethlehem, the place where he had once met a young couple, weary from their journey, seeking only a place to rest.

Cassius closed his eyes, his mind drifting back to that night. He remembered Mary's face—the exhaustion, the determination, the way she had looked at Joseph with love and trust. He remembered offering them shelter, seeing their relief as they settled for the night. The memory of Mary's hopeful eyes as she rested her hand on her swollen belly had stayed with him, a vivid reminder of the fragility of hope amidst hardship. He had thought of them often in the weeks that followed, wondering if they had found what they were looking for, if they had found a place to rest, a place to bring their child into the world. And now, as he stood there, the scroll with Herod's orders lying on the table behind him, he felt a chill run down his spine.

Could it be them? Could the child Herod sought be the same one Mary had carried—the one she had protected so fiercely, her eyes filled with hope as she looked to the future?

Cassius turned away from the window, his heart pounding, his breath coming in short, uneven gasps. He felt a knot tighten in his chest, a sense of dread that he could not shake. He had followed orders his entire life—he had done what was asked of him, without question, without hesitation. But this—this was something he could not bring himself to do.

He crossed the room, his eyes falling on the scroll once more. He reached out, his fingers brushing against the parchment, the words seeming to burn into his skin. He could see the faces of the children in his mind—innocent, helpless, their lives cut short before they had even begun. He could see the faces of their mothers, their fathers, the grief, the terror. He could see Mary's face, her eyes filled with hope for her child, and he knew that he could not be the one to extinguish that hope. He could not be the one to bring darkness upon such innocence.

Cassius took a deep breath, his hands trembling as he rolled the scroll back up, his mind racing. He had a choice to make—a choice that could cost him everything. He could follow Herod's orders, lead his men to Bethlehem, and carry out the massacre. Or he could walk away, turn his back on everything he had known, everything he had fought for, and try to find another way.

He thought of his men, the soldiers who had fought beside him, who had trusted him to lead them. He thought of their loyalty, their belief in him. They would follow him, no matter what he commanded. They would march to Bethlehem, they would carry out the orders, and they would live with the weight of it for the rest of their lives. He could not do that to them. He could not ask them to carry the burden that he himself could not bear.

Cassius unrolled the scroll once more, his eyes scanning the words, his mind made up. He could not do it. He could not be the one to lead this massacre, to bring death to innocent children. He would not be Herod's pawn, not in this. He would find another way—he had to.

He crossed the room, his heart pounding as he pushed open the door, stepping out into the cool morning air. The sky was painted in shades of pink and gold, the first light of day breaking over the horizon. He could hear the distant call of a rooster, the soft rustle of the wind in the trees. The world seemed so peaceful, so quiet, and yet he knew that darkness was gathering, that a storm was about to break.

Cassius made his way through the barracks, his footsteps echoing in the silence. He could see his men, still resting, their faces peaceful, unaware of the orders that lay waiting for them. He paused, his eyes scanning the room, his heart heavy with the weight of what he was about to do.

"Marcus," he called softly, his voice barely more than a whisper.

A young soldier stirred, his eyes blinking open as he looked up at Cassius, his brow furrowed in confusion. "Centurion?" he asked, his voice thick with sleep.

"Get up," Cassius said, his voice steady, his eyes locked on the young man. "We need to talk."

Marcus rose to his feet, his eyes wide with concern as he followed Cassius out of the barracks, the cool morning air waking him fully. "What is it, sir?" he asked, his voice filled with apprehension.

Cassius took a deep breath, his eyes meeting Marcus's, his voice steady. "We have received orders from Herod," he said, his voice low. "We are to march to Bethlehem. We are to kill every male child under the age of two."

Marcus's eyes widened, his face paling as he took a step back, his heart pounding in his chest. "But... but why?" he asked, his voice trembling. "What threat could children possibly pose?"

Cassius shook his head, his heart heavy. "The king fears a prophecy," he said, his voice filled with bitterness. "He fears a child who has been born, a child who is said to be the Messiah. He will do whatever it takes to protect his throne, even if it means spilling innocent blood."

Marcus was silent, his eyes filled with horror as he looked at Cassius. "What are we going to do?" he asked, his voice barely more than a whisper.

Cassius took a deep breath, his eyes filled with determination. He thought of Mary, of her vulnerability and courage, and of the child she had carried. He could not allow that light to be extinguished. "We are not going to Bethlehem," he said, his voice steady. "We are not going to follow these orders. I will not lead my men into a massacre. I will not be a part of this.""

Marcus stared at him, his heart pounding, his mind racing. "But... but what about Herod? What will he do when he finds out?"

Cassius looked away, his eyes drifting to the horizon, the first light of dawn breaking over the hills. "I don't know," he said, his voice filled with uncertainty. "But I do know that I cannot do this. I cannot be the one to take the lives of innocent children. If that means defying Herod, then so be it."

Marcus swallowed, his heart filled with fear, but also with a sense of admiration. He had followed Cassius for years, had trusted him, had believed in him. And now, as he looked at the man before him, he knew that he would follow him still, no matter the cost.

"What do you need me to do?" Marcus asked, his voice steady, his eyes filled with determination.

Cassius looked at him, a small smile tugging at the corners of his lips. "Gather the men," he said, his voice filled with resolve. "We leave before the sun is fully up. We will not go to Bethlehem. We will not follow these orders."

Marcus nodded, his heart pounding as he turned and hurried back into the barracks, his mind racing. Cassius watched him go, his heart filled with a mixture of fear and hope. He knew the risks, knew the danger they faced in defying Herod. But he also knew that he could not betray the memory of Mary and her child, could not lead his men into something so dark, so wrong. He had seen hope in Mary's eyes, and he would do everything in his power to protect that hope.

He turned his eyes to the horizon, the sun rising slowly, its light spilling over the hills, bathing the world in a soft, golden glow. He took a deep breath, his heart swelling with determination. He would not be a part of Herod's madness. He would not let fear dictate his actions.

For the first time in a long time, Cassius felt a sense of peace, a sense of purpose. He knew that the road ahead would be difficult, that there would be challenges, dangers he could not yet imagine. But he also knew that he was doing the right thing, that he was choosing light over darkness, hope over fear.

And as the sun continued to rise, Cassius turned and walked back into the barracks, his heart filled with resolve, ready to face whatever lay ahead.

CHAPTER 25: FLIGHT TO EGYPT (PART I)

Joseph knew they were in danger. The angel's message had been unmistakable—Herod's men would come, and they had to flee. The night was dark, the sky heavy with thick clouds that blotted out the stars. The flickering light of the lantern cast long shadows across the stable walls, its glow just barely illuminating the worn wooden beams. Joseph stood at the entrance, his brow furrowed, his breath visible in the cold air as he peered into the blackness beyond. His heart pounded, the fear from the dream still gripping him tightly.

The dream he had just woken from lingered vividly in his mind, its message as clear as the chill that seeped into his bones, each beat of his heart echoing the urgency of the angel's words. "Get up. Take the child and his mother and flee to Egypt," the angel's voice had commanded, its urgency cutting through the haze of sleep. The presence of the angel had been overwhelming—its form radiant, its voice resonating deep within Joseph's soul, filling him with both awe and fear. There had been no mistaking the warning—danger was coming. Herod's reach was closing in on them, and if they stayed, their son's life would be in peril.

Joseph turned back, his eyes locking on Mary, who was kneeling beside the makeshift cradle, her fingers lightly brushing Jesus' cheek as he slept. The baby stirred slightly, a soft sigh escaping his lips, and Mary smiled, her heart swelling with love. She shifted slightly, her shoulders tensing, her gaze filled with both love and a hint of apprehension. She looked up as Joseph approached, her eyes immediately catching the tension etched into his face.

In the corner of the stable, Miriam watched with concern, her hands clasped tightly together. Her heart heavy with worry. The stable had been a refuge, and leaving it meant stepping into a world full of uncertainty. She took a deep breath, determined to do whatever she could to help them.

Beside Miriam, Leah and Salome exchanged glances, their expressions mirroring each other's unease. Leah stepped forward, her voice soft as she spoke. "Joseph, we will help you however we can," she said, her eyes earnest. Salome nodded in agreement, her hand resting on Miriam's shoulder as if to lend her strength. They all knew that this night marked the beginning of a perilous journey, but their resolve to protect the young family was unwavering.

"Joseph?" she whispered, her voice barely audible, yet laced with concern. "What is it?"

He knelt beside her, his hand resting gently on her shoulder. "We have to go, Mary," he said, his voice trembling slightly. "We have to leave. Tonight. I had a dream. An angel spoke to me. Herod knows about the child. He will send his men. We have to flee. To Egypt.""

Mary's breath caught in her throat, her heart pounding in her chest as the weight of his words sank in. Her hands began to tremble, her fingers tightening around the blanket that covered Jesus. Her gaze dropped to Jesus, his tiny form peaceful in sleep, and fear gripped her like a vice, her pulse quickening, her stomach twisting in knots. She looked back at Joseph, her eyes wide, searching his face for reassurance.

"Egypt?" she asked, her voice cracking. "So far away... How will we get there?"

Joseph swallowed, his own fears bubbling beneath the surface, but he forced himself to stay calm. "We'll manage, Mary. We have to. I will keep you both safe. The angel said to leave immediately—under the cover of night. We must go now, while there's still time."

Mary nodded, her heart heavy with fear but also with trust. She knew Joseph would protect them, knew that he would do whatever it took to keep their family safe. She took a deep breath, her hand moving to rest over Joseph's, her eyes filled with determination. "Then we will go. Whatever it takes, we will go."

Joseph rose to his feet, his movements quick, purposeful. The creak of the wooden floor echoed through the stable, mingling with the soft rustle of hay underfoot. He began gathering what little they had—a few scraps of food, a blanket, the small pouch of coins they had managed to save. The cold air bit at his fingers as he worked, each sound amplified in the stillness of the stable. Mary, her hands trembling, wrapped Jesus in a thick cloth, holding him close to her chest as he stirred, his tiny eyes blinking open, oblivious to the fear that gripped his parents. The wind outside howled softly, slipping through the gaps in the wooden slats, adding to the sense of urgency as they prepared to leave.

Miriam stepped forward, placing a gentle hand on Mary's arm. "I wish I could come with you," she whispered, her voice filled with emotion. "But I know you must go alone. Just know that you have our prayers, always." Mary looked at Miriam, her eyes glistening, and nodded. "Thank you, Miriam. For everything."

Leah moved closer, her gaze resting on Jesus. She knelt beside Mary, her fingers brushing the infant's hand. "We will spread the word of his birth, quietly, among those we trust," she promised. Salome joined her, her eyes locking on Mary's. "This child is special, and we will do our part to protect him, even from afar."

The stable was cold, the wind slipping through the gaps in the wooden slats, biting at their skin. Joseph led the way, his eyes scanning the darkness as they stepped outside, his heart pounding in his chest. The village of Bethlehem was quiet, the streets empty, the only sound the distant barking of a dog, the rustling of leaves in the wind.

Mary held Jesus close, her steps careful as she followed Joseph, her heart pounding with each step. She glanced back at the stable, the place where they had welcomed their son into the world, and she felt a pang of sorrow. It had been humble, rough, but it had been their refuge, the place where their miracle had happened. Now, they were leaving it behind, stepping into the unknown, driven by the need to protect the precious life she held in her arms. A part of her heart remained with that place—the birthplace of her child, the first place they had been a family. She whispered a silent goodbye, her eyes glistening as she turned away, knowing they could never return.

Joseph led them down the narrow path that wound through the village, his eyes darting from side to side, his ears straining for any sign of movement. Every shadow seemed to hold a threat, every rustle of the wind made his heart jump. Suddenly, a faint noise—a snap of a twig—made him freeze, his breath catching in his throat. He stood still for a moment, his heart pounding, before slowly exhaling when the sound didn't repeat. He knew Herod's men could be anywhere, that they could come at any moment, and the fear of what might happen if they were caught gnawed at him.

Behind them, Miriam watched from a distance, her heart aching with worry. She remained hidden in the shadows, watching until she could no longer see them. Beside her, Leah and Salome stood silently, their hands clasped in prayer. "May God guide them and keep them safe," Salome whispered, her voice breaking. Leah nodded, her eyes glistening as they turned away, heading back toward the village, their hearts heavy but filled with hope.

"We need to move quickly," Joseph said, his voice low as he glanced back at Mary. He could see the fear in her eyes, the way her arms tightened around Jesus, but he also saw her strength, the determination that burned within her. A silent prayer formed in his mind—'Lord, protect us, guide our steps.' She nodded, her lips pressed into a thin line, and together they pressed on, their steps quickening as they made their way toward the edge of the village.

The road ahead was dark, the path barely visible beneath the canopy of trees that lined the way. The trees loomed above them, their branches twisting like skeletal hands against the night sky. The air was thick with the scent of damp earth, and the rustle of leaves whispered around them, adding to the sense of isolation. Joseph led Mary along the winding road, his hand gripping hers, his heart pounding as they moved further away from the village, from everything they had known. The weight of the journey ahead pressed down on him—the uncertainty, the danger—but he pushed it aside. All that mattered was getting Mary and Jesus to safety.

As they moved further from Bethlehem, the landscape began to change, the road becoming rougher, the trees more sparse. The night was quiet, the only sound the crunch of their footsteps on the dirt path, the rustle of the wind through the branches. The cold seeped into their bones, but they kept moving, their breaths visible in the frigid air.

Mary glanced down at Jesus, her heart swelling with love and fear. His eyes were closed, his tiny hand curled around her finger, and she felt a surge of protectiveness, a fierce determination to keep him safe no matter what. She looked at Joseph, his face set with resolve, and she knew they would make it, no matter how far they had to go.

Hours passed, the darkness deepening as they traveled. The landscape around them was desolate, the road stretching out endlessly before them. They were alone, the vastness of the night pressing down on them, but they pressed on, their hearts filled with the knowledge that they were doing what they had to do, that they were following the will of God. Mary closed her eyes briefly, her thoughts turning to her faith—'Lord, give us strength. Guide our steps and keep us safe.' It was this faith that kept her moving, even when exhaustion threatened to overtake her.

The first light of dawn began to break over the horizon, a soft glow spreading across the sky, and Joseph paused, rubbing his eyes, wincing from the fatigue that had settled deep in his bones. His eyes scanned the landscape ahead. He could see the faint outline of hills in the distance, the path winding through the valley below. He turned to Mary, his eyes filled with concern, his voice soft as he spoke.

"We need to find a place to rest," he said, his eyes drifting to Jesus, who was still nestled against Mary's chest. "We've traveled far, and you both need to sleep. There's a grove of trees just ahead—we can rest there until nightfall, then continue on."

Mary nodded, her body aching from the long journey, her arms heavy from holding Jesus close. She could feel the exhaustion settling in, the weight of the night pressing down on her, but she knew they couldn't stop for long. They had to keep moving, had to stay ahead of the danger that was surely following them.

Joseph led her to the grove, the trees offering a small measure of shelter from the wind. The ground beneath them was uneven, the cold earth pressing against their feet, and the wind whistled through the branches above, a haunting reminder of the isolation they faced. He spread out the blanket he had brought, his hands gentle as he helped Mary sit, his eyes filled with concern as he looked at her, at the baby in her arms.

"Rest, Mary," he said, his voice soft, his hand brushing a stray lock of hair from her face. "I will keep watch. You and Jesus need to rest."

Mary nodded, her eyes heavy as she leaned back against the trunk of the tree, her arms cradling Jesus close. She closed her eyes, her heart filled with a mixture of fear and hope, the weight of the journey ahead pressing down on her, but she knew they would make it. They had to. God was with them, guiding them, protecting them.

Joseph watched as Mary's breathing slowed, her eyes closing as she drifted into an exhausted sleep. He looked down at Jesus, his tiny face peaceful, his breaths soft and steady. Joseph's heart swelled with love, with a fierce protectiveness that made his chest ache. He knew the road ahead would be difficult, that there would be challenges, dangers they could not yet imagine. But he also knew that he would do whatever it took to keep them safe. 'No matter what comes,' he thought, 'I will not fail them. I will not let fear take hold.'

The sun rose slowly, the light spreading across the landscape, bathing the world in a soft, golden glow. Joseph kept watch, his eyes scanning the horizon, his heart filled with determination. They would make it. They would reach Egypt. They would keep their son safe, no matter the cost.

And as the morning turned to afternoon, the world around them seemed to hold its breath, the quiet of the grove broken only by the rustle of the wind in the leaves, the distant call of a bird. They were alone, the three of them, but they had each other, and for now, that was enough. Joseph glanced at Mary, her eyes still closed in sleep, and reached out to gently take her hand. He squeezed it softly, a silent promise that he would always be by her side. Mary stirred slightly, her fingers curling around his, and a faint smile touched her lips even as she slept. In that small moment of tenderness, Joseph felt his resolve strengthen—they would face whatever lay ahead, together.

CHAPTER 26: THE MASSACRE BEGINS

The dawn sky was a soft shade of gray, the sun still a faint promise on the horizon. Bethlehem was just beginning to stir, the quiet streets still drowsy with sleep. The clatter of wooden shutters being opened echoed through the narrow alleys, mingling with the low voices of women greeting each other from doorways, and the occasional bark of a dog. Life carried on, unaware of the storm about to break.

Suddenly, the tranquility shattered. Roman soldiers stormed the streets, their heavy boots pounding on the cobblestones, their swords glinting with a deadly gleam. They moved with ruthless precision, kicking in doors, dragging out families, and searching for young boys. The screams of terrified mothers filled the air, their voices raw with desperation as they clung to their children, their faces twisted with fear.

Miriam stood in her small kitchen, her hands busy kneading a lump of dough for the day's bread. The warmth of the fire crackled beside her, the aroma of yeast mingling with the scent of herbs hanging from the beams above. She worked the dough rhythmically, her mind drifting to thoughts of the young family who had stayed in her stable—the woman, Mary, and her newborn child, whose arrival had filled her with an unexpected hope.

She was startled from her thoughts by the sound of distant shouting. Her hands froze, her eyes narrowing as she listened, her heart picking up its pace. The voices grew louder, the shouts becoming clearer, and a chill ran down her spine as she heard the unmistakable clang of metal—soldiers.

Miriam wiped her flour-dusted hands on her apron, moving quickly to the small window at the front of her house. She peered out, her breath catching in her throat as she saw them—dozens of soldiers, their faces hard, their swords gleaming in the morning light. They moved through the street with purpose, their voices sharp as they barked orders, the clatter of their armor a discordant symphony that shattered the quiet of the morning.

Her heart lurched as she saw one of the soldiers push a man to the ground, his sword drawn, the man's cries echoing through the narrow street. Another soldier grabbed a small child by the arm, the boy's screams piercing the morning air. The mother lunged forward, her face streaked with tears, her nails clawing at the soldier's arm as she fought to free her child. The soldier responded with a brutal backhand, sending her sprawling to the ground, blood trickling from her split lip.

Panic gripped Miriam, her breath coming in short, shallow gasps as she turned away from the window, her mind racing. She didn't know what they were looking for, but she knew it wasn't good. She could feel the fear in the air, the tension that seemed to thicken with every passing moment.

The door burst open, and her husband, Ezra, stumbled in, his face pale, his eyes wide with terror. "Miriam," he gasped, his voice trembling. "The soldiers—they're killing the children. They're looking for boys—young boys."

Miriam's heart dropped, her stomach twisting with fear. "The children?" she whispered, her voice barely audible. "But why? What do they want with them?"

Ezra shook his head, his hands trembling as he grabbed her arm, his eyes filled with desperation. "It's Herod. He's ordered it. He thinks a king has been born here, a threat to his throne. He wants them all gone, Miriam—all of them."

Miriam felt her knees go weak, her heart pounding in her chest as she tried to comprehend what he was saying. The image of Mary's child flashed in her mind, the memory of his tiny face, so innocent, so full of life. Her hands trembled as she gripped the edge of the table, her eyes wide with fear.

"We have to do something," she said, her voice trembling, her eyes locking with Ezra's. "We can't just stand here—we have to help them."

Ezra hesitated, his eyes filled with fear. "What can we do, Miriam? We have no power against Herod's soldiers. They are armed, ruthless. If they catch us—"

Miriam shook her head, her eyes fierce, her heart pounding with a mixture of fear and determination. "We can't just stand by and watch, Ezra. We have to try—if we can save even one child, it will be worth it."

The shouts grew louder, the sound of a woman's scream piercing the air, and Miriam felt her heart clench, her breath catching in her throat. She moved to the door, her hands trembling as she pushed it open, her eyes scanning the street. She could see the soldiers now, moving from house to house, their swords drawn, their faces cold, emotionless.

A woman stumbled out of her house, her face streaked with tears, her arms empty. She fell to her knees in the street, her cries echoing through the narrow alley, her voice filled with a grief that tore at Miriam's heart. One of the soldiers approached her, his face twisted in a sneer. He grabbed her by the hair, yanking her head back, his voice a harsh growl as he barked at her to be silent. She whimpered, her eyes filled with pain, her body trembling.

Miriam knew, in that moment, that there was no time to waste.

"Come on," Miriam said, her voice filled with urgency as she grabbed Ezra's arm, pulling him toward the door. "We have to go—now."

Ezra followed her, his heart pounding, his mind racing as they stepped out into the chaos of the street. The air was thick with fear, the cries of mothers and children echoing around them, the clatter of soldiers' armor a constant reminder of the danger that surrounded them.

Miriam moved quickly, her eyes scanning the street, her heart pounding as she searched for any sign of the children, for any chance to help. She spotted a young boy, his face streaked with tears, his small body trembling as he crouched behind a stack of firewood, his eyes wide with terror.

Without hesitation, Miriam moved toward him, her hands gentle as she reached out, her voice soft, soothing. "It's alright, little one," she whispered, her heart breaking at the fear in his eyes. "I'm here to help you."

The boy looked up at her, his eyes filled with confusion, with fear, but he didn't move, didn't resist as she pulled him into her arms, holding him close as she turned to Ezra, her eyes filled with urgency.

"We have to get him out of here," she said, her voice trembling. "We have to find a place to hide him."

Ezra nodded, his eyes scanning the street, his heart pounding as he spotted a narrow alleyway, half-hidden behind a stack of crates. "This way," he said, his voice low, his eyes locking with Miriam's. "Hurry."

They moved quickly, their steps careful, their eyes darting from side to side, the sounds of chaos all around them. Miriam held the boy close, her heart aching at the feel of his small body trembling against hers, his soft sobs muffled against her shoulder.

They slipped into the alley, the shadows providing a small measure of cover, the noise of the street fading slightly as they moved further from the main road. Ezra led the way, his eyes scanning the narrow passage, his heart pounding with fear, with desperation.

Miriam's breath came in short, shallow gasps, her arms aching from holding the boy, her heart pounding as they moved further into the shadows. She could hear the soldiers in the distance, their voices sharp, their movements methodical as they searched each house, each alley, leaving no stone unturned.

They reached the end of the alley, the narrow passage opening up into a small courtyard, half-hidden behind a crumbling stone wall. Ezra turned to Miriam, his eyes filled with determination, his voice low. "We can hide him here," he said, his eyes drifting to an old storage shed, its door hanging loosely on its hinges. "It's not much, but it might be enough."

Miriam nodded, her heart pounding as she moved toward the shed, her eyes scanning the small space, her heart swelling with both fear and hope. She set the boy down, her hands gentle as she brushed the hair from his face, her eyes filled with warmth, with love.

"Stay here, little one," she whispered, her voice trembling. "Stay quiet, stay hidden. We will come back for you. I promise."

The boy looked up at her, his eyes wide, filled with tears, but he nodded, his small body trembling as he curled up in the corner of the shed, his eyes never leaving Miriam's. She felt her heart break, her breath catching in her throat as she closed the door, her eyes lingering on the boy for a moment before she turned away, her heart heavy.

Ezra was waiting for her, his eyes filled with worry, his hand resting gently on her arm. "We have to go, Miriam," he said, his voice soft, his eyes filled with pain. "There are others—others who need our help."

Miriam nodded, her heart aching as she turned away from the shed, her eyes scanning the street, her mind filled with the faces of the children, with the cries of their mothers, the weight of the moment pressing down on her. She knew that they couldn't save everyone, but they had to try. Every child they could hide, every mother they could comfort, would be worth the risk. She glanced at Ezra, her eyes fierce with determination, and they moved back into the fray—driven by hope, driven by love, and unwilling to let fear be their master.

CHAPTER 27: CASSIUS' DEFIANCE

The sun had barely risen, its rays still weak against the heavy chill of dawn, when Cassius heard the first cries echo across the narrow streets of Bethlehem. He stood at the edge of the village, his hand resting on the hilt of his sword, his heart pounding in his chest. The orders had been clear—find the boys, no older than two years, and leave no survivors. It was an order that had made his stomach churn, but he had nodded, his face expressionless, a soldier bound by duty.

Cassius had not chosen to be here. He had been forced, ordered to join the detachment sent to Bethlehem. He had always been loyal, a man who followed orders, but he had known from the moment he heard Herod's command that this was different. There was no honor in this mission, no glory to be gained—only the screams of the innocent and the blood of children.

But now, as he heard the cries of mothers, the pleading voices, the sound of lives being torn apart, something deep inside him twisted in revolt. He had fought battles, had faced enemies in the heat of war, had spilled blood in the name of Rome. But this was different. This was not war. This was slaughter, and his heart recoiled at the very thought of it.

The cries grew louder, the chaos drawing nearer, and Cassius turned, his eyes scanning the street. He saw his fellow soldiers moving with grim determination, their faces set, their swords glinting in the morning light. He could see the fear in the eyes of the villagers, the desperation as they tried to shield their children, to hide them, to save them.

His gaze caught on a family—a mother, her face pale, her eyes wide with terror, her arms wrapped protectively around her young son. The boy's face was pressed against her chest, his small hands clinging to her tunic, his eyes squeezed shut. The father stood in front of them, his arms outstretched, his voice pleading as he faced the soldier advancing toward them, his sword drawn.

Cassius felt his heart lurch, his breath catching in his throat. He could see the fear in the father's eyes, the desperation, the love that drove him to stand in front of his family, even when he knew it would not be enough. The soldier moved closer, his sword raised, and Cassius felt something snap inside him.

"Stop!" he shouted, his voice ringing out, cutting through the chaos. He moved forward, his hand gripping the hilt of his sword, his heart pounding in his chest. The soldier turned, his eyes narrowing as he looked at Cassius, confusion crossing his face.

"What are you doing, Cassius?" the soldier demanded, his voice sharp, his eyes flicking to the family, then back to Cassius. "These are Herod's orders. We are to leave no child alive."

Cassius shook his head, his jaw clenched, his eyes filled with determination. "No," he said, his voice steady, his heart pounding. "I will not be a part of this. I will not harm the innocent."

The soldier's eyes widened, his face twisting with anger. "You defy Herod? You would risk your life for these people?"

Cassius stepped closer, his eyes locked on the soldier's, his voice low, filled with conviction. "I cannot do this," he said, his voice trembling slightly. "This is not justice. This is not honor. I will not harm those who cannot defend themselves."

The soldier stared at him for a long moment, his eyes filled with disbelief, then with fury. He took a step back, his grip tightening on his sword, his voice filled with venom. "You are a fool, Cassius. Herod will have your head for this."

Cassius didn't flinch, his eyes steady, his heart pounding. "So be it," he said, his voice unwavering. "I would rather die than be a part of this massacre."

The soldier sneered, his eyes narrowing. "You are no longer one of us," he spat, his voice dripping with contempt. He turned, his eyes scanning the street, his voice rising. "Cassius is a deserter! He defies Herod's orders!"

Cassius felt his heart pound, his breath catching in his throat as he looked at the family, the fear in their eyes. He moved quickly, his hand resting on the mother's shoulder, his voice urgent. "Go," he whispered, his eyes locking with hers. "Take your son and run. Do not look back."

The mother hesitated for a moment, her eyes wide with fear, then she nodded, her eyes filling with tears as she looked at Cassius, her voice trembling. "Thank you," she whispered, her voice barely audible.

Cassius nodded, his heart heavy as he watched them disappear down the narrow alley, the mother holding her child close, the father following close behind. He turned back, his eyes scanning the street, his heart pounding. He knew what he had done, knew the price he would pay, but he also knew that he could not have done anything else.

The sound of footsteps drew closer, the shouts of his fellow soldiers echoing through the narrow streets, and Cassius knew that his time was running out. He moved quickly, his heart pounding, his eyes scanning the street for any sign of an escape. He could hear the soldiers behind him, their voices filled with anger, with the promise of retribution.

He slipped into a narrow alley, his breath coming in short,

shallow gasps, his heart pounding in his chest. He knew he could not outrun them, knew that they would find him, but he had to try. He had made his choice, had chosen to protect the innocent, to stand against the darkness, even if it meant his own death.

The alley was dark, the walls closing in around him, the sound of the soldiers growing louder, their footsteps echoing off the stone walls. Cassius pressed on, his breath ragged, his heart pounding, his eyes searching for any way out, any chance to escape.

He turned a corner, his eyes locking on a small door, half-hidden behind a stack of crates. He moved toward it, his hands trembling as he pushed it open, slipping inside, his breath coming in short, shallow gasps. The room was dark, the air thick with dust, the only light coming from a small window high on the wall.

Cassius leaned against the door, his heart pounding, his mind racing. He knew he couldn't stay here, knew that they would find him, but for a moment, he allowed himself to catch his breath, to gather his thoughts. He had made his choice, had chosen to defy Herod, to stand for what was right, and he would face whatever came next.

The sound of footsteps grew louder, the shouts of the soldiers echoing through the alley, and Cassius knew that his time was running out. He moved toward the window, his hands trembling as he climbed onto the crates, his heart pounding in his chest. He pushed the window open, the cold air hitting his face, the sound of the village in chaos echoing around him.

He climbed through the window, his feet hitting the ground with a thud, his eyes scanning the street. He could see the soldiers now, their faces twisted with anger, their swords drawn, their eyes searching for him. He took a deep breath, his heart pounding, his eyes locking on the path ahead.

He ran, his feet pounding against the ground, his breath coming in short, ragged gasps. He could hear the soldiers behind him, their shouts growing louder, their footsteps echoing in his ears.

He pushed himself harder, his heart pounding, his eyes focused on the path ahead.

The village was in chaos, the cries of the mothers, the shouts of the soldiers, the clatter of swords all blending together in a cacophony of fear and despair. Cassius moved through the streets, his heart heavy, his mind filled with the faces of the innocent, with the memory of the family he had helped, with the knowledge of what he had done.

He turned a corner, his eyes locking on the edge of the village, the open desert beyond. He could see the hills in the distance, the promise of freedom, of escape. He pushed himself harder, his breath coming in short, ragged gasps, his heart pounding in his chest.

The sound of footsteps grew closer, the shouts of the soldiers echoing in his ears, but Cassius didn't look back. He knew that he might not make it, that the soldiers might catch him, that he might pay the ultimate price for his defiance. But he also knew that he had done what was right, that he had stood for the innocent, that he had chosen to protect rather than destroy.

And as he ran, the desert stretching out before him, the sun rising over the hills, Cassius felt a sense of peace, a sense of purpose. He had made his choice, had chosen to stand for what was right, and whatever came next, he knew he could face it with a clear conscience.

The cries of the village faded behind him, the chaos of Bethlehem left in the distance as Cassius ran toward the horizon, his heart pounding, his eyes focused on the path ahead. He had defied Herod, had chosen to protect the innocent, and though he knew the price would be steep, he also knew that he had done what was right.

And for Cassius, that was enough.

CHAPTER 28: FLIGHT TO EGYPT (PART II)

The night was deep and moonless as Joseph led Mary and Jesus along the dusty path, the sounds of the desert carrying only the whispers of their hurried steps. The chill of the night air wrapped around them, and Mary pulled her shawl tighter over her shoulders, glancing down at Jesus cradled in her arms. His breathing was steady, the rhythm comforting, a small beacon of peace amid the fear that gripped her heart.

"Keep moving," Joseph whispered, his voice barely audible over the soft rustle of the wind in the dry grass. He glanced behind them, his eyes scanning the darkness for any sign of danger. Every shadow seemed to move, every distant sound a threat. He could still hear the cries of Bethlehem in his ears, the chaos they had left behind, and the weight of the danger pressed on his chest.

Mary looked up at the sky, her eyes searching for the familiar glow that had led them before—the star that had shone so brightly, marking the way. For a moment, her heart stilled, her breath catching in her throat, until she saw it again, low on the horizon, a gentle shimmer of light. It was almost as if it beckoned them onward, promising safety, a divine reminder that they were not alone.

"Look," Mary whispered, nudging Joseph gently and nodding toward the star. He looked up, and in that moment, the tension in his shoulders seemed to ease, his eyes softening as he saw the light. They were not navigating this journey blindly; they had a guide.

The landscape around them was barren, the sand stretching out into the darkness, broken only by sparse clusters of shrubs and the jagged shapes of rocks. The path ahead was unclear, winding and twisting, and Joseph led them with careful steps, each movement deliberate, his senses on high alert. The weight of responsibility bore down on him—he had to protect them, had to get them to safety.

The journey was fraught with peril. The night seemed endless, the vast desert a labyrinth of unseen dangers. Every sound was magnified in the silence—distant howls that could have been the wind or wild animals, the rustle of movement from unseen creatures. Once, they heard the unmistakable snap of a twig, and Joseph's heart froze, his body tensing as he held his breath, waiting for what might come. His eyes narrowed, scanning the darkness for the source of the sound. But then, silence returned, leaving only the pounding of his heart in his ears.

Suddenly, a noise—a rustle from behind a nearby cluster of rocks—made Joseph freeze, his hand instinctively reaching for the staff at his side. He stepped in front of Mary, his eyes narrowing as he peered into the darkness, his heart pounding. Mary held her breath, pulling Jesus closer, her eyes wide, her ears straining for any sound.

A figure emerged from the shadows, moving slowly, hands raised in a gesture of peace. It was a man, cloaked, his face obscured by the hood of his robe. He moved with deliberate slowness, his voice soft as he spoke. "Do not be afraid," he said, his tone gentle, reassuring. "I mean you no harm."

Joseph's grip on his staff tightened, his eyes wary. "Who are you?" he asked, his voice low, his stance protective.

The stranger lowered his hood, revealing a weathered face, his eyes kind, a gentle smile tugging at his lips. "My name is Benjamin," he said. "I am a traveler, like you. I know the paths through these lands, and I have seen the soldiers. They will not be far behind."

Mary's breath caught, her eyes locking with Joseph's, fear flickering in her gaze. The stranger continued, his voice filled with urgency. "I know a way—through the hills, a path that they will not think to follow. You must trust me."

Joseph hesitated, his eyes searching the stranger's face, looking for any hint of deception. But there was none—only sincerity, a quiet determination. He glanced at Mary, and she nodded, her eyes filled with hope. "We have no choice," she whispered. "We must keep Jesus safe."

Joseph nodded, his eyes meeting Benjamin's. "Lead the way," he said, his voice firm, his heart pounding with a mixture of fear and hope.

Benjamin turned, moving swiftly, his steps sure and confident. Joseph and Mary followed, their feet crunching softly on the sandy ground, the chill of the night air biting at their skin. The path wound upward, the hills rising steeply, the terrain rocky and uneven. Mary stumbled, her steps faltering, and Joseph was there in an instant, his arm around her, steadying her.

"I'm alright," she whispered, her voice filled with determination, her eyes fixed ahead. She could see the glow of the star above, its light filtering through the darkness, guiding them onward.

They moved in silence, the only sound the soft rustle of their robes, the distant call of a night bird echoing across the empty expanse. Time seemed to blur, the minutes stretching into hours, each step bringing them closer to safety, yet the fear never fully left their hearts. They were vulnerable, alone, fugitives in a land that offered no sanctuary.

As they climbed higher, the landscape opened up, the desert stretching out below them, bathed in the faint glow of the approaching dawn. Benjamin led them to a small alcove, a hollow in the hillside, hidden from view. "Rest here," he said, his voice gentle, his eyes filled with understanding. "The soldiers will not find you. I will keep watch."

Joseph nodded, his eyes filled with gratitude. "Thank you," he said, his voice thick with emotion. "We owe you our lives."

Benjamin shook his head, his smile gentle. "You owe me nothing," he said. "I am only doing what is right. There is something about this child—something that must be protected." He glanced at Jesus, his eyes softening, and for a moment, his expression seemed almost awed.

Mary sank to the ground, her body aching with exhaustion, her heart heavy with the weight of the journey. She looked down at Jesus, his face peaceful, his small hand curled against her chest, and a tear slipped down her cheek. She brushed it away quickly, her eyes lifting to meet Joseph's.

"We will make it," she whispered, her voice filled with determination.

Joseph knelt beside her, his hand resting gently on her shoulder, his eyes filled with love. "We will," he said, his voice steady. "As long as we have each other, we will make it."

The night wore on, the sky shifting from black to deep blue, the first hints of dawn painting the horizon in shades of pink and gold. The air was still, the world quiet, and for a moment, it felt as though time itself had stopped, the weight of their fear lifted by the promise of a new day.

Benjamin stood at the edge of the alcove, his eyes scanning the horizon, his posture alert. He turned, his gaze meeting Joseph's, a small smile playing at his lips. "The worst is over," he said, his voice soft, his eyes filled with reassurance. "You are safe—for now."

Joseph nodded, his heart swelling with gratitude. He looked at Mary, her eyes closed, her breathing steady, Jesus still cradled in her arms. He reached out, his fingers brushing against her cheek, his heart filled with love, with hope, with the promise of the future they would build together.

They had faced the darkness, had fled from the danger, and though the road ahead was still uncertain, they knew that they would not face it alone. They had each other, their faith, and the guidance of a light that had never wavered.

As the first rays of sunlight broke over the hills, bathing the world in golden light, Joseph felt a sense of peace, a sense of hope that filled his heart, pushing aside the fear that had gripped him for so long. They had made it through the night, had found a way to safety, and for now, that was enough.

Mary stirred, her eyes fluttering open, her gaze lifting to meet Joseph's. She smiled, her eyes filled with love, and in that moment, Joseph knew that they would be alright. They had made it this far, had faced the darkness together, and they would continue to face whatever lay ahead, with faith and love.

As the sun fully emerged over the horizon, its warmth spread across the barren landscape, dispelling the lingering shadows of the night. The desert, once foreboding, now seemed softened, its stark beauty illuminated by the golden light. It was a new day—a new beginning.

Mary shifted Jesus gently in her arms, feeling the weight of him, both literal and symbolic. He was small, yet immense in significance. His presence was a reminder of why they continued, why they endured. She glanced at Joseph, her expression filled with unspoken gratitude and unshakable resolve.

Joseph rose to his feet, his eyes scanning the distant path ahead. He didn't know what challenges still awaited them in the unknown lands of Egypt, but his spirit remained unbroken. Turning back to Mary, he extended a hand, helping her rise. Together, they were stronger. Together, they would protect what was most precious.

Benjamin, standing watch as ever, gave them one final glance.

"Your journey is not yet over," he said, his tone quiet but firm. "But remember, the greatest strength lies not in avoiding the darkness, but in carrying the light through it."

Mary and Joseph both nodded, the truth of his words settling deep within them. With a final farewell, Benjamin stepped back, allowing them to move forward, their steps purposeful despite the weariness in their bones.

As they began to walk, the desert around them seemed alive with possibility, the landscape stretching endlessly yet invitingly toward a future they could not yet see. Each step was a declaration of faith, a testament to love, a refusal to give in to fear.

Behind them, the night lingered only as a memory. Ahead, the dawn grew brighter, promising more than survival—it promised hope.

And in the center of it all, the child slept, his presence a quiet assurance that the journey was not in vain. He was the light they carried, the reason they pressed on.

Together, they would face whatever came. Together, they would find their way. And with each passing moment, the desert gave way to a horizon that seemed a little closer, a little more radiant.

For as long as the light guided them, they knew they would never be truly lost.

CHAPTER 29: THE MAGI'S RETURN

Azar watched as the distant outline of his homeland came into view, his heart heavy with emotions he couldn't quite name. The endless dunes of sand stretched out like a golden sea, meeting the horizon in a seamless embrace. The familiar scent of myrrh and spices filled the air, and a warm breeze whispered against his face, carrying with it the sounds of the bustling city that awaited him. His journey had been long and filled with wonder, but now, as he returned, Azar knew that everything had changed.

He looked over at his companions—Melchior and Balthazar—who rode beside him, their camels moving in a steady rhythm, their faces lined with fatigue. They had traveled together for many months, guided by a star that had led them to Bethlehem, to a humble stable where they had found a child who was more than any king they had ever seen. That child, lying in a manger, surrounded by the love of his parents, had filled Azar's heart with a sense of peace and purpose he had never known.

"Azar," Melchior called, his voice breaking through Azar's reverie. "Are you prepared to tell them? Will they believe us?"

Azar turned, meeting Melchior's gaze, his eyes filled with uncertainty. "I do not know," he replied, his voice low. "But we must try to share what we have seen." It is a truth that must be shared."

Melchior nodded, a small smile tugging at his lips. "Yes," he said, his voice soft. "A truth that must be shared."

As they approached the gates of their city, Azar could feel the weight of what he was about to do. The people here were proud, steeped in traditions that had stood for centuries. Would they listen to the story of a child born in a distant land, in a stable of all places? Would they understand the significance of what they had witnessed, of the prophecy fulfilled? He could only hope.

The streets were alive with the energy of the day—vendors calling out their wares, children running through the narrow alleys, laughter and voices filling the air. Azar dismounted, his feet touching the warm earth, his eyes scanning the faces of the people around him. He could see the curiosity in their eyes, the whispers as they noticed his return. He had left on a mysterious journey, and now his return carried an aura of change that made people pause.

Azar's father, a respected elder, stood at the entrance of their home, his eyes narrowing as he took in his son's weary form. He stepped forward, his voice carrying both relief and questioning. "Azar, my son," he said, his hands resting on Azar's shoulders. "You have returned. Tell me, what have you found on your journey? What is it that has changed you so?"

Azar took a deep breath, his heart pounding, his voice trembling slightly as he spoke. "Father," he said, his eyes locking with his father's, "I have seen something that has changed me forever. I have seen the child who will bring hope to the world. The Messiah—the King of Kings."

The crowd that had gathered around them fell silent, the air thick with tension, curiosity etched on every face. Azar's father frowned, his voice cautious. "A child? What do you mean, Azar?"

Azar spoke, his voice growing stronger with each word, his heart filling with the memory of that night in Bethlehem. He spoke of the star that had appeared in the sky, the journey they had undertaken, the joy and awe they had felt when they found the child, wrapped in swaddling clothes, lying in a manger. He described the humble stable, the love in the eyes of the child's mother, the divine light that seemed to fill the space.

The people listened, their eyes wide, their hearts torn between disbelief and hope. They had heard of prophecies, of a Messiah who would come to bring peace, but to hear that it had happened, that a child had been born in a distant land—it was almost too much to take in.

Azar's father shook his head, his voice filled with skepticism. "A king born in a stable? A Messiah lying in a manger? How can this be, Azar? How can such a great thing happen in such a humble place?"

Azar stepped closer, his voice steady. "Father, I know it is hard to believe. But I saw him, and I felt it in my heart. This child is the one we have been waiting for.""

There was a long silence, the people looking at one another, their faces filled with uncertainty, their hearts struggling to accept what they had heard. Then, slowly, one of the elders stepped forward, his eyes filled with curiosity. "You say you saw a sign? A star that led you to this child?"

Azar nodded, his voice soft, his eyes filled with emotion. "Yes," he said. "A star, brighter than any I have ever seen. It led us across the desert, guided us to that place. It was as if the heavens themselves were showing us the way."

The elder nodded slowly, his eyes thoughtful, his voice filled with wonder. "Perhaps," he said, his voice barely a whisper, "perhaps there is more to this than we can understand. Perhaps the light has indeed come, and we must open our hearts to it."

Azar felt a surge of hope, his eyes shining as he looked around at the faces of the people, their expressions softening, their hearts beginning to open to the possibility of what he had seen, of the hope that had been born among them.

Melchior stepped forward, his voice rising above the murmurs, filled with urgency, with hope. "We have traveled far," he said, his eyes locking with the people around him. "We have seen the truth, and we have come to share it. This child is the one who will bring peace, who will bring light to the darkness. We must not turn away from this truth."

The people began to murmur among themselves, their eyes filled with wonder, their hearts beginning to open. Azar watched as they spoke, his heart pounding. He had chosen to leave behind his comfort to spread the word of the Messiah.

His father looked at him, his eyes filled with a mixture of pride and uncertainty, his voice soft. "You truly believe this, my son?"

Azar nodded, his voice trembling. "Yes, Father. I believe it. This child is the one who will guide us.""

There was a long moment of silence, the people gathered around them, their eyes wide, their hearts beginning to open. Azar knew this was just the beginning of their journey. He knew that this was just the beginning, that the journey ahead would be filled with challenges, with doubts, but he also knew that they were not alone. They had the light of the Messiah to guide them, to give them hope.

As the sun began to set, casting its golden light over the city, Azar knew that he had found his purpose. He would spread the word, would share the light, would bring hope to those who needed it most. The journey had only just begun, but he was ready to face whatever lay ahead, with faith and hope.

The light had come, and their world was forever changed.

CHAPTER 30: MARY'S REFLECTION

The desert air was heavy with warmth, the scent of dry earth and distant greenery mingling together in a strange yet comforting way. Mary sat beneath the shade of a solitary date palm, her eyes turned towards the horizon where the sun was beginning its descent, painting the sky in golden hues. She held her son close, feeling the gentle rise and fall of his chest as he rested, the rhythmic sound of his breathing blending with the whisper of the wind.

The journey to Egypt had been long and uncertain, filled with moments of fear, hope, joy, and exhaustion. There were times when Mary had felt her strength falter, when the weight of the responsibility she bore had seemed too much to carry. But each time she had looked at the child in her arms, she had felt her heart swell with a strength she had not known she possessed. He was her purpose, her reason for every sacrifice.

The small clearing around her was quiet, the world seemingly holding its breath in the cool of the evening. Joseph was not far, tending to the fire they had built, his back turned as he worked. Mary watched him for a moment, her heart filled with gratitude. He had been her rock, her anchor through the storm. His quiet strength had carried her through the darkest nights, his gentle touch a constant reminder that she was not alone.

She looked down at her son, his tiny hand curled against her chest. He was so innocent, so pure. The angel had called him the Messiah, had said he was destined to bring salvation, to be the light that would guide the world. But in this moment, he was simply her son—a baby who needed warmth and love, who found comfort in her embrace.

Mary took a deep breath, her eyes turning once more to the horizon, her mind drifting to all that had come before—the whispers of the villagers in Nazareth, the fear that had gripped her when she first realized what had been asked of her. She had been so young, so unprepared for the weight of it all. But she had trusted, had believed in the promise given to her, in the divine plan that was unfolding.

And now, here they were, in a foreign land, far from home, far from the life she had once known. The sacrifices they had made weighed heavily on her heart, each one a reminder of the path they had chosen. She missed her family, the familiar faces and places of Nazareth. She missed the comfort of her own home, the laughter of friends, the simple joy of a life unburdened by the weight of prophecy.

But she would not trade this journey. For in the midst of all the uncertainty, there was a deep and abiding peace, a sense of purpose that went beyond anything she had ever known. She had been chosen to bring this child into the world and protect him. And she would do so, no matter the cost, no matter the sacrifices.

"Mary?" Joseph's voice broke through her thoughts, gentle and familiar. She looked up, her eyes meeting his as he approached, his face softened by the glow of the setting sun. "The fire is ready. Come, you should eat something."

Mary smiled, nodding as she shifted her son in her arms. He looked tired, but his eyes held a warmth that filled her with peace.

"Thank you, Joseph," she said softly, her voice filled with

emotion. She stood, cradling the baby close as she walked towards the fire, the warmth of the flames a welcome comfort against the chill of the desert evening.

Joseph reached out, his hand resting gently on her shoulder, his eyes searching hers. "Are you all right?" he asked, his voice barely a whisper.

Mary nodded, her heart filled with love for him. "I am," she said, her voice steady. "I was just thinking… about everything. About how far we've come, about what lies ahead."

Joseph's eyes softened, his hand moving to rest against her cheek, his thumb brushing gently against her skin. "We will face it together," he said, his voice filled with conviction. "Whatever comes, we will face it together."

Mary closed her eyes, her heart swelling with emotion as she leaned into his touch. She took a deep breath, the warmth of Joseph's hand and her son in her arms grounding her with peace.

"Yes," she whispered, her voice barely audible over the crackle of the fire. "Together."

They sat by the fire, sharing a simple meal, the warmth of the flames casting flickering shadows around them. The desert stretched out beyond, vast and endless, a reminder of the journey still ahead. But for now, in this moment, they were safe, they were together, and that was enough.

Mary looked down at her son, his eyes open, gazing up at her with curious innocence. She smiled, her heart swelling with love as she cradled him closer, her lips brushing against his forehead.

The baby cooed softly, his tiny hand reaching up to touch her face, his eyes filled with wonder. Mary closed her eyes, her heart filled with overwhelming love. She had been chosen for this, had been given this gift, this responsibility, and she would cherish it, every moment, every sacrifice.

The night deepened, stars appearing and twinkling against the darkness. Mary looked up, her eyes tracing the constellations, her heart filled with a sense of awe. There was a plan, a purpose to all of this, a divine hand guiding their path, and she would trust in that, would find her strength in that.

Joseph reached for her hand, his fingers intertwining with hers, his eyes meeting hers across the fire. He smiled, his love for her evident in every line of his face, in every gentle touch.

"We will find our way," he said softly, his voice filled with hope. "No matter where this journey takes us, we will find our way."

Mary nodded, her heart swelling with emotion, her eyes filling with tears. She looked down at her son, knowing in her heart that they would be all right. That they would face whatever came, that they would find their way, together.

She took a deep breath, her eyes turning to the horizon as dawn began to touch the sky. The journey ahead was uncertain, the road filled with challenges, but she was ready. For she had her son, she had Joseph, and she had her faith.

For they were together, and that was all that mattered.

CHAPTER 31: THE LIGHT OF BETHLEHEM

The desert wind whispered softly through the narrow alleyways of Bethlehem, rustling the fronds of the date palms and carrying with it the distant echoes of a bustling market. In a small house nestled among the ancient stone buildings, a family gathered around a flickering oil lamp, their eyes reflecting the golden glow of the flame. Miriam, the innkeeper's wife, sat with her young granddaughter on her lap, her eyes crinkled with warmth as she began to tell the story.

"It was a long time ago, my love," Miriam began, her voice gentle yet resonant, "on a night when the stars were brighter than ever before. Your great-grandmother helped a young couple find shelter in a humble stable, and there, amidst the hay and the animals, something miraculous happened."

The little girl leaned closer, her eyes wide with wonder. "A baby was born, right?" she asked, her voice barely a whisper, as if afraid to break the magic of the story.

Miriam smiled, nodding as she gently brushed a strand of hair away from the child's face. "Yes, my dear. A baby who would bring light to the world. His name was Jesus, and that night, the stable glowed with the light of hope, love, and promise."

The room seemed to hold its breath as Miriam continued, her words weaving a tapestry of that night—the weary parents, Mary and Joseph, their faith unwavering despite the hardships they faced, the shepherds who had arrived breathless with awe, and the wise men who had journeyed from distant lands, drawn by a star that shone brighter than any other.

"The light that was born that night," Miriam said softly, her eyes glistening, "was not just for those who were there. It was for all of us, for every heart that longs for hope, for every soul that needs comfort." She looked down at her granddaughter, her heart swelling with love. "And that light, my darling, is still with us today."

The little girl gazed up at her grandmother, her small hand resting against Miriam's chest. "Can we see the light, Grandma?" she asked, her eyes filled with innocent curiosity.

Miriam's smile deepened, and she shook her head gently. "It's not a light we see with our eyes," she said, her voice a mere whisper. "It's a light we carry here." She placed her hand over her granddaughter's heart. "It's in the way we love each other, the way we help those in need, the way we forgive even when it's hard. It's the light that guides us when we feel lost."

The little girl closed her eyes, as if trying to feel the warmth of that light within her. Miriam watched her, her heart swelling with both love and hope. She had seen so much in her life—the cruelty of men, the hardships of survival—but she had also seen moments of pure, selfless love, acts of kindness that shone like beacons in the darkness. And that, she knew, was the true miracle of that holy night—the light that continued to spread, even after all these years.

Across town, Eli sat by a fire, the flames dancing before him, their warmth seeping into his bones. He had gathered with other shepherds, some of whom had been with him that night, others who had grown up hearing the story. His voice was strong as he spoke, the story spilling from his lips with the same passion and conviction as it had the first time.

"The child born in that stable brought a promise," Eli said, his eyes glancing around the circle of faces illuminated by the firelight. "A promise that we are not alone, that we are loved beyond measure. It was a promise not just for kings and priests, but for shepherds like us, for every single person, no matter who they are."

The shepherds nodded, some with tears glistening in their eyes. Eli's heart swelled with the memory of that night—the angels, the singing, the awe that had filled him as he looked upon the baby lying in a manger. It had changed him, shaped his life in ways he was still discovering, even now.

Eli had become a leader among the shepherds, sharing the story of that night with anyone who would listen. Each year, on the anniversary of Jesus's birth, they gathered, sharing stories, reaffirming their faith, and reminding one another of the light that continued to guide them. The simple act of gathering around the fire, of speaking of hope and love, had become a cherished tradition—a symbol of the enduring bond they shared.

In a distant land, Azar, one of the wise men, sat beneath the vast, starry sky, his gaze turned to the heavens. The journey he had taken so long ago had been one of faith, of seeking something greater than himself, and he had found it in the eyes of a newborn child, in the humility of a stable, in the faith of those who had welcomed him.

"The light born that night," Azar said, his voice carried on the wind, "is like the stars above. It may seem small from afar, but it is endless, eternal. It guides us, reminds us of what truly matters. It is the light of love, of sacrifice, of redemption."

He looked at his companions, their faces reflecting the glow of a small fire they had kindled. "And it is up to us to carry that light, to let it shine in our hearts, to share it with those who are lost in the darkness."

The men nodded, their hearts filled with the same sense of purpose that had driven them to follow the star all those years ago. They had returned to their homeland, but the journey had not ended. It had only just begun. And as long as they lived, they would continue to share the light, to let it shine in every corner of the world.

Back in Bethlehem, Leah stood at the edge of the village, her eyes on the horizon, the first light of dawn just beginning to break. She had spent her life helping others, inspired by what she had witnessed in that humble stable. She had seen the face of hope, had held it in her arms, and it had changed her forever.

She closed her eyes, a smile spreading across her face as she felt the warmth of the morning sun on her skin. The light born that night had never dimmed, not in her heart, not in the hearts of those she had touched. It had grown, spread, become a beacon for those in need, a reminder that love was the greatest power of all.

Leah took a deep breath, her heart filled with gratitude for the journey she had been on, for the light she had been given to carry. She knew that her work was far from over, that there were still so many who needed to hear the story, who needed to feel the warmth of the light. And she would continue, for as long as she lived, she would continue to share the hope that had been born that night, the love that had been given to all of them.

Cassius, once a soldier bound by orders, had found a new purpose in Bethlehem. He had stayed, choosing to dedicate his life to acts of service, to caring for those in need. The weight of his past actions still haunted him, but each day he chose to do good, to be better. There were moments of doubt, of despair, when the memories of what he had done threatened to consume him. But in those moments, he remembered the light he had witnessed, the hope that had been born that night, and it gave him the strength to carry on.

One day, as he helped rebuild a neighbor's home, Cassius felt a sense of peace he had never known before. He realized that redemption was not a destination but a journey—one he would walk for the rest of his life. And with every act of kindness, every selfless gesture, he felt the darkness within him recede, replaced by the warmth of the light he had chosen to carry.

The sun rose higher, its rays spreading across the village, touching each stone, each tree, each heart. And as Leah stood there, watching the new day begin, she knew that the light of Bethlehem would never fade. It would continue to shine, to guide, to heal, to bring hope to a world that so desperately needed it.

For that was the true miracle of that holy night—the light that had come into the world, a light that could never be extinguished, a light that lived on in each of them, in every act of kindness, every moment of love.

And as long as there were hearts willing to carry it, the light of Bethlehem would continue to shine, touching lives across generations, bringing hope to every corner of the world.

Miriam, Eli, Azar, Leah, Salome and Cassius—they were just a few of the countless lives that had been touched by the light born that night. Each of them carried it in their own way, shared it in their own words, their own actions. And though their stories were different, their purpose was the same—to let the light shine, to let the hope spread.

And as the years turned into decades, as the story of that night was passed down from one generation to the next, the light of Bethlehem continued to grow, to touch hearts, to change lives.

It was a light that could never be extinguished, a promise that would never be broken, a love that would never fade.

And as long as there were those willing to carry it, to share it, to let it shine, the light of Bethlehem would continue to illuminate the world, a beacon of hope, of love, of redemption.

The story was far from over. It was only just beginning.

✼ ✼ ✼

AFTERWORD

As the final pages of *The Light of Bethlehem* come to a close, I want to take a moment to reflect on the enduring themes that have driven this story—the themes of hope, love, and the light that shines even in the darkest moments. This book is not just a recounting of an ancient event but an invitation to consider the miracles that exist within all of us.

The story of Bethlehem is about more than a single night or a single event. It's about the resilience of the human spirit, the sacrifices we make for love, and the simple acts of kindness that ripple across generations. It reminds us that extraordinary things often come from the humblest of places and that hope can find a way even when the path seems impossible.

In writing this book, my hope was to share a perspective that allows the reader to connect with the humanity behind the well-known story—the people whose courage, doubt, and faith made it all possible. These are emotions and experiences we all share, even today, and they form the common threads that connect us to those who lived long ago.

I hope that *The Light of Bethlehem* has brought warmth to your heart, has inspired you to look at the world a little differently, and has reminded you of the light that each of us carries. May we all be inspired by the love and grace found in this story to shine our own light, no matter how small it may seem, into the lives of those around us.

Thank you for joining me on this journey. May the light of Bethlehem guide your steps, fill your days with wonder, and bring you peace.

ACKNOWLEDGEMENT

Writing *The Light of Bethlehem* has been an extraordinary journey, and it wouldn't have been possible without the support, guidance, and encouragement of so many wonderful people.

First and foremost, my deepest gratitude goes to my wife, Subhashini, whose unwavering belief in me and tireless support have been my guiding light. To my daughter, Sasha, your boundless curiosity and joyful spirit remind me each day of the beauty in every story and the importance of sharing light with the world.

I want to thank my family and friends, who encouraged me at every stage of this process. Your patience, insightful feedback, and constant inspiration have been instrumental in shaping this book.

To my co-creators and collaborators, thank you for sharing your talents, knowledge, and creativity so generously. Your contributions have added layers of depth and richness to the story that would not have been possible otherwise.

A heartfelt thank you to my readers. Your love for stories that touch the heart, your willingness to explore both the known and unknown, and your passion for hope and light are what inspired this book. This work is for you, and I hope it brings the magic and warmth of Bethlehem into your lives.

Finally, I would like to express my appreciation for all

the writers, historians, and artists who have spent lifetimes bringing history to life and shedding light on the stories that shape our world. Your dedication has been a guiding inspiration throughout this creative journey.

ABOUT THE AUTHOR

D. Deckker

Dinesh Deckker is a seasoned expert in digital marketing, boasting more than 20 years of experience in the industry. His strong academic foundation includes a BA in Business Management from Wrexham University (UK), a Bachelor of Computer Science from IIC University (Cambodia), an MBA from the University of Gloucestershire (UK), and ongoing PhD studies in Marketing.

Deckker's career is as versatile as his academic pursuits. He is also a prolific author, having written over 100+ books across various subjects.

He has further honed his writing skills through a variety of specialized courses. His qualifications include:

Children Acquiring Literacy Naturally from UC Santa Cruz, USA
Creative Writing Specialization from Wesleyan University, USA
Writing for Young Readers Commonwealth Education Trust
Introduction to Early Childhood from The State University of New York
Introduction to Psychology from Yale University
Academic English: Writing Specialization University of

California, Irvine,
Writing and Editing Specialization from University of Michigan
Writing and Editing: Word Choice University of Michigan
Sharpened Visions: A Poetry Workshop from CalArts, USA
Grammar and Punctuation from University of California, Irvine, USA
Teaching Writing Specialization from Johns Hopkins University
Advanced Writing from University of California, Irvine, USA
English for Journalism from University of Pennsylvania, USA
Creative Writing: The Craft of Character from Wesleyan University, USA
Creative Writing: The Craft of Setting from Wesleyan University
Creative Writing: The Craft of Plot from Wesleyan University, USA
Creative Writing: The Craft of Style from Wesleyan University, USA

Dinesh's diverse educational background and commitment to lifelong learning have equipped him with a deep understanding of various writing styles and educational techniques. His works often reflect his passion for storytelling, education, and technology, making him a versatile and engaging author.

BOOKS BY THIS AUTHOR

The Magic Of Christmas: 10 Short Stories To Brighten Your Holiday

Discover the magic, warmth, and joy of the holiday season with this heartwarming collection of Christmas short stories. The Magic of Christmas brings together ten enchanting tales designed to remind readers of the beauty of love, generosity, and togetherness. Each story captures the true spirit of Christmas, celebrating unexpected kindness, rekindled friendships, and the simple joys of giving and receiving.

Mindful Christmas: Practices For A Joyful Holiday

Are you ready to transform your holiday season into a time of peace, connection, and joy? Mindful Christmas is your guide to creating a meaningful and stress-free celebration through the power of mindfulness.

Mary Magdalene: Apostle Of The Apostles

For centuries, Mary Magdalene has been one of the most misunderstood figures in Christian history. Often mischaracterized as a repentant sinner, her true role in the early Christian movement was far more profound. In Mary Magdalene: Apostle of the Apostles, Dinesh Deckker uncovers the historical Mary Magdalene—a devoted disciple, the first witness to the resurrection, and a key figure in the foundation of

Christianity.

Nighttime Wonders: 30 Bible Tales For Little Hearts

Nighttime Wonders: 30 Bible Tales for Little Hearts is a heartwarming collection of Bible stories, perfect for children aged 3-5. Each story is written in simple, calming language, making it ideal for bedtime reading. From Creation to the life of Jesus, these short stories introduce your child to the love, wisdom, and wonders of the Bible.

Agape: The Love Of Jesus And The Heart Of Christianity

Discover the life-changing power of Agape—the selfless, unconditional love that Jesus taught and modeled throughout His life. In Agape: The Love of Jesus and the Heart of Christianity, Dinesh Deckker explores how this divine love can transform our relationships, communities, and even the world. Through rich insights drawn from Scripture, personal stories, and practical guidance, Deckker demonstrates how embracing Agape can heal wounds, build bridges, and bring peace to a divided world.

The Birth Of Jesus: A Heartwarming Christmas Story For Children

In The Birth of Jesus, authors Dinesh Deckker & Subhashini Sumanasekara bring the Christmas story to life for children ages 5-10. Follow Mary, Joseph, and baby Jesus in this heartwarming tale as they journey to Bethlehem and welcome visitors who come bearing gifts of love and joy. Through gentle storytelling and engaging illustrations, young readers will experience the magic of the first Christmas, making this book a cherished keepsake for the holiday season.

Made in the USA
Columbia, SC
22 January 2025